MRS. JEFF[RIES]
SOMETHING ODD . . .

From the hall, Mrs. Jeffries heard the sound of footsteps. She straightened and smoothed her long skirt just as the door opened and Inspector Witherspoon appeared.

"Mrs. Jeffries," he said in surprise. "What on earth are you doing here?"

"Finding your cigar case," she replied, pulling the case out of her skirt pocket and handing it to him. "I realized this morning when I handed you your coat that it wasn't in the pocket. I thought you must have lost it when you were here yesterday."

"Gracious me," he exclaimed, staring at the case with a puzzled frown. "I didn't even know it was missing."

"Do you know, it's the most curious thing," Mrs. Jeffries said.

"What is?"

"I found the case beneath this medicine cabinet. The corner was sticking out. It must have slipped out of your pocket while you were searching the room yesterday, but when I went to pick it up, I found this as well." She handed the piece of cork to him. "Isn't that odd?"

#1

MORE MYSTERIES FROM THE
BERKLEY PUBLISHING GROUP...

MELISSA CRAIG MYSTERIES: She writes mystery novels—and investigates crimes when life mirrors art. "Splendidly lively."
—*Publishing News*

by Betty Rowlands

A LITTLE GENTLE SLEUTHING	FINISHING TOUCH
OVER THE EDGE	EXHAUSTIVE ENQUIRIES

TREWLEY AND STONE MYSTERIES: Even the coziest English villages have criminal secrets...but fortunately, they also have Detectives Trewley and Stone to dig them up!

by Sarah J. Mason

MURDER IN THE MAZE	CORPSE IN THE KITCHEN
FROZEN STIFF	DYING BREATH

INSPECTOR KENWORTHY MYSTERIES: Scotland Yard's consummate master of investigation lets no one get away with murder. "In the best tradition of British detective fiction!" —*Boston Globe*

by John Buxton Hilton

HANGMAN'S TIDE	TWICE DEAD
FATAL CURTAIN	RANSOM GAME
PLAYGROUND OF DEATH	FOCUS ON CRIME
CRADLE OF CRIME	CORRIDORS OF GUILT
HOLIDAY FOR MURDER	DEAD MAN'S PATH
LESSON IN MURDER	DEATH IN MIDWINTER
TARGET OF SUSPICION	

THE INSPECTOR AND MRS. JEFFRIES: He's with Scotland Yard. She's his housekeeper. Sometimes, her job can be murder...

by Emily Brightwell

THE INSPECTOR AND MRS. JEFFRIES	THE GHOST AND MRS. JEFFRIES
MRS. JEFFRIES DUSTS FOR CLUES	MRS. JEFFRIES TAKES STOCK
MRS. JEFFRIES ON THE BALL	MRS. JEFFRIES ON THE TRAIL
MRS. JEFFRIES PLAYS THE COOK	

SCOTLAND YARD MYSTERIES: Featuring Detective Superintendent Duncan Kincaid and his partner, Sergeant Gemma James... "Charming!"
—*New York Times Book Review*

by Deborah Crombie

A SHARE IN DEATH	ALL SHALL BE WELL

THE INSPECTOR
AND
MRS. JEFFRIES

EMILY BRIGHTWELL

BERKLEY PRIME CRIME, NEW YORK

THE INSPECTOR AND MRS. JEFFRIES

A Berkley Book / published by arrangement with the author

PRINTING HISTORY
Berkley edition / February 1993

ISBN: 0-425-13622-1

A BERKLEY BOOK ® TM 757,375
Berkley Books are published by The Berkley Publishing Group,
200 Madison Avenue, New York, New York 10016.
The name "BERKLEY" and the "B" logo
are trademarks belonging to Berkley Publishing Corporation.

PRINTED IN THE UNITED STATES OF AMERICA

10 9 8 7 6 5 4

This book is dedicated to ROBERT G. ARGUILE.
*Thanks for all the encouragement, help,
and the always delightful visits
to our side of the pond.*

THE INSPECTOR
AND
MRS. JEFFRIES

CHAPTER 1

Dr. Bartholomew Slocum was definitely dead. Inspector Gerald Witherspoon stared morosely at the body slumped over the huge mahogany desk and fervently wished he were home sitting in front of a roaring fire instead of standing in a gloomy Knightsbridge surgery.

From behind him, he heard Constable Barnes clear his throat. Witherspoon thrust the image of a cozy fire and a glass of port out of his mind and remembered his duty. Straightening his spine, he moved determinedly toward the body.

Aware of the two pairs of eyes staring at his back, Witherspoon leaned forward and examined the dead man. It was not a chore he relished. The fact was, he was rather squeamish about dead people, but as corpses went, this was a rather nice one. At least it wasn't covered in blood.

He heard an impatient shuffle of feet behind him, and that brought him back to the problem at hand. "Hmmm," he muttered thoughtfully, trying to sound both wise and official. "The gentleman is definitely dead."

"Yes, we know," said Dr. Sebastian Hightower somewhat irritably. "That is, of course, why I summoned the police."

"Hmm, yes." Witherspoon turned and smiled faintly at the portly man standing next to Constable Barnes. Hightower didn't return his smile. He gazed impatiently

1

from beneath thick brown eyebrows and pointedly picked up his watch chain.

"The doctor was obviously reading when death occurred," Witherspoon said. "See how his head is resting on that book. Except for the rather peculiar way his arms are flopped out, one on each side, you'd think he was merely taking a nap."

"Well he isn't napping," snapped the doctor, glaring at Witherspoon. "He's dead and the circumstances are very suspicious."

"Suspicious?" Witherspoon echoed. He didn't think there was anything suspicious about a dead person in a doctor's surgery. Mind you there were more dead people in hospitals, but surely, if one couldn't die in a hospital, a surgery was the next best place.

"Look, Inspector, I do wish you'd get on with it. You've been here ten minutes and all you've done is stare at the fellow."

Witherspoon stiffened. He was terribly unsure of what to do, but he wouldn't tolerate the fact that it was starting to show. "Staring at the corpse, as you call it," he said cooly, "is the best way to begin an investigation. We don't even know that Dr. Slocum's death is a matter for the police. Now, Dr. Hightower, could you please describe how you came to find the deceased?"

Hightower sighed. "I've already told all that to your constable here."

"I'm sure you have, but I'd like to hear it myself."

"I came in and saw Dr. Slocum slumped over his desk. At first I thought he was doing exactly as you said, taking a nap. But when he didn't move after I'd called out several times, I realized something was wrong. I examined him quickly and checked for a pulse, then realized he was dead. But it was when I saw what he had clutched in his other hand that I decided to send for the police. Luckily, the butler happened to come in then, so I sent him for the constable on the corner."

"I see," Witherspoon muttered. He was annoyed with himself. He hadn't even realized Dr. Slocum *was* holding something in his fingers. Looking down, he saw a small vial curled in the palm of the dead man's hand.

"Precisely. Uh . . . exactly why did you think this vial warranted such an action? I mean, why did it strike you as suspicious? The gentleman's dead, but there certainly isn't any sign of violence. Perhaps the poor man has had a heart attack."

"Inspector Witherspoon," Hightower began slowly, as though talking to a thick-skulled child, "if you'll trouble yourself to lift Dr. Slocum's head, you'll see why I considered his death suspicious."

Witherspoon swallowed hard and rolled the dead man's head to one side. He tried not to shudder as a pair of open, beady gray eyes gazed up at him. The face surrounding those eyes was puffed up like bread dough, and the flesh was flushed a bright pink. A hideously swollen tongue protruded from between lips that had been stretched in a horrible parody of a smile.

Inspector Witherspoon quickly turned the face away and stepped back.

"As you can see, he's swelled up like a bullfrog," Hightower continued. "He may well have actually died of heart failure, but I assure you, it was brought on by something else. I summoned the constable because of the vial in his hand. That's Syrup of Ipecac, man, it's got one use and one use only. An emetic. Dr. Slocum's been poisoned. Furthermore, I suspect he knew it and was attempting to treat himself when he died."

"Right, right, well, the police surgeon will be here shortly, and I'm sure he'll concur with your opinion."

Hightower snorted and reached up to stroke his full brown beard.

"How did you happen to be here today? Did you have an appointment with the deceased?" Witherspoon was sure that was an appropriate question.

"My being here was merely a matter of chance."

"Chance?"

"Yes." Hightower shifted his walking stick from one hand to the other. "Actually, I had an appointment with a patient who lives around the corner, but as I was early, I thought I'd call in on Dr. Slocum. He didn't see patients on Wednesdays. I decided to pop in and say hello. We hadn't seen each other in a good while—"

"He didn't see patients on Wednesdays?" Witherspoon interjected, sure that was a pertinent point.

"No," Hightower replied, "he did not." He stared at the inspector curiously. Was the man going to repeat everything he said? "His surgery was closed on Wednesdays. But as I was saying before you interrupted, I thought I'd call in, but when I knocked on the door, there was no answer. I thought that was a bit peculiar, but as there was nothing I could do about it, I went on round to my patient's."

"Why did you find it peculiar?"

Hightower, who wasn't the most patient of men, took a deep, calming breath. "Because there was no one home, that's what was peculiar." He lifted his hand in a wide arc. "Look at this place. The house does not run by itself. Dr. Slocum had a full staff. Cook, footmen, a housekeeper, two maids and a butler. There should have been some-one here."

"Perhaps he gave them all the afternoon off," suggested the inspector. He too had servants, and if the weather was fine and his house was in tip-top shape, he frequently gave them all the whole day off.

Hightower was shaking his head vigorously. "No, he wouldn't have done that. Slocum was much too worried about thieves to give the entire staff the day out. Why, the man always made sure there were at least two footmen on the premises when he took his servants and went to his farm in Essex."

"You certainly are well versed in how the late Dr. Slocum ran his household," Witherspoon said. "You must have been very close friends. Can you tell me——"

"We certainly weren't close friends," Hightower interrupted. He looked as though he'd been insulted. "The entire neighborhood knew every dull detail of his domestic arrangements. He was always boasting about how efficiently he managed things. Just last Saturday he was out in the gardens at Mrs. Crookshank's afternoon tea bragging to everyone about how clever he was. Bored everyone to tears too. That's why I'm so familiar with the way he ran his household." Hightower paused to take a breath.

"Yes, I can see your point. So you're sure that Dr. Slocum wouldn't have given the servants a day off as a special holiday? Perhaps a treat for a job well done."

"I don't think so," Hightower replied, looking a bit uncertain. "I know for a fact that he split their days out. Said it was more efficient that way."

"More efficient, you say?"

"Yes." Hightower's cheeks began to turn red. "Some of the staff got Wednesday afternoons off and the rest got Saturday afternoons off. Someone should have been here."

Witherspoon nodded. "If no one answered the door, how did you get in?"

Hightower looked annoyed. "I got in through the back door."

"Through the back door? But I thought no one was home?"

"There wasn't anyone home," the doctor snapped. "I told you, I was visiting another patient and she lives around the corner. That means she shares the communal gardens on this block. After I finished examining her, she asked me to take a look at her rose bushes. They've got blight. I do have some small renown for growing exceptional roses myself. While I was checking her plants, I happened to glance up and noticed Dr. Slocum's back door was open. Naturally, I came to investigate. For Heaven's sake, man, I've told all this to the constable."

"Yes, yes, I'm sure you have, but——"

"Look, Inspector," Dr. Hightower pulled his pocket watch out again and scowled, "I really must be off. If you've more questions, you can come see me at my surgery in Harley Street."

There were a lot of questions the inspector knew he should ask, but he couldn't quite remember what they were. Thank goodness he'd be able to go home soon. He could think better on a full stomach, and furthermore, he could always think better after a nice chat with Mrs. Jeffries, his housekeeper.

"That'll be fine, Dr. Hightower," Witherspoon said quickly. "Just leave your address with Constable Barnes."

The inspector decided he'd better do as the doctor suggested and get on with it. The fact that he was totally at a loss as to what to do next didn't deter him. He frowned and tried to remember something his housekeeper had said recently. Oh yes, it was about that dreadful business in the Kensington High Street . . . Now what was it? His face brightened as it suddenly came to him. "If you'd been in charge from the first, Inspector," Mrs. Jeffries had said emphatically, "you wouldn't have made the silly mistakes Inspector Nivens made. Why, you'd have searched the murder scene yourself and not left it up to a constable!"

Of course, of course. That's what he'd do next.

Witherspoon walked the length of the room, his footsteps muffled by the thick Persian carpet. He glanced down, noting the rich, muted colors of the rug, and thought that it was awfully fancy for a surgery. His gaze swept the room. The walls were painted white and the windows covered by tied-back green velvet curtains. Floor-to-ceiling shelves and bookcases filled one wall, and along the opposite wall there was a row of cabinets with a variety of vials and bottles of all different colors and shapes. The doctor's heavy mahogany desk was in the center of the room, and at the far end, there was a dressing screen next to the examination table.

Except for the fact it was a bit more opulent than his own physician's surgery, Witherspoon could see nothing out of the ordinary.

He crossed the hall, went into the dining room and walked quickly to the end of the table where the remains of Dr. Slocum's luncheon were sitting on a silver tray.

Witherspoon stared at the table but could see nothing unusual. A crumpled white linen napkin lay next to an empty wine bottle. He reached down and picked up the crystal goblet the deceased had drunk from, and noticed that there was a bit of wine still in the bottom of the glass.

"Are you ready to see the butler yet?" Constable Barnes called from the doorway.

"In a moment," Witherspoon replied, setting the goblet next to a dirty plate littered with lamb chop bones. He picked up a soup bowl and saw that there was a bit of mushroom soup left in the bottom. Sighing, he glanced up at the constable, who was still waiting in the hall. "You'd better find a box, Constable," he said. "This might be evidence, so we'd better send the whole lot off to the Yard for examination."

"You think he might have been poisoned, then?" Barnes asked.

"There is always the possibility," Witherspoon replied. "I'd better have a word with the butler now."

Wendell Keating, a small mouse-like man with a wispy white mustache and watery blue eyes, stood waiting in the drawing room, his fingers clutched together in front of him.

Witherspoon advanced toward the servant. "Good afternoon, I'm Inspector Witherspoon from Scotland Yard and I've a few questions to ask you."

"Yes, sir, I'm sure you do."

"You know of course, that Dr. Slocum was found dead this afternoon in his surgery?"

The butler nodded but said nothing.

"We think he's been poisoned." Witherspoon watched Keating's reaction carefully, but the butler's rigid features didn't change. "What do you think of that?"

"That's terrible, sir." The servant's voice was flat.

"It certainly is." Witherspoon allowed himself a brief smile. "And it's our job to find out how it happened."

"Yes, sir."

"Now, why was the household deserted this afternoon?"

"Dr. Slocum gave us the afternoon off."

"But I have it on good authority that Dr. Slocum's regular habit was to give half the staff Wednesday off and the other half Saturday. Are you saying he gave you all the afternoon off at the same time?"

"Yes."

"Why?"

"I don't know."

Witherspoon began to get annoyed. "Had he ever done it before?"

"Yes."

"Well, when?"

Keating shrugged. "Sometimes. I don't rightly recollect when the last time was. But occasionally, he up and gave everyone the afternoon off at the same time. It didn't do no good to ask him why; he wasn't one for telling his reasons."

Further inquiry continued in the same vein, with Witherspoon asking every question that popped into his head and the butler answering precisely what was asked and volunteering no more. By the time the inspector ran out of questions, his head was starting to ache.

He did remember to ask the butler where he'd been that afternoon, though. But that answer didn't help him very much. Keating had spent the afternoon visiting a sick friend in Kew. Witherspoon duly recorded the information and then dismissed the butler.

The inspector was tired, hungry and confused. Surely the information he'd received meant something, but what? He decided to wait until he received the police surgeon's report before he did anything else. Perhaps Dr. Hightower was wrong. Maybe the doctor hadn't been poisoned after all.

Even if he had, Witherspoon told himself as he marched into the hall and reached for his overcoat, that didn't mean he'd been murdered. Accidental poisonings certainly weren't unheard of.

Barnes met him in the hallway. "Do you want me to keep a constable here all night, sir?"

"All night?" Witherspoon frowned, wishing he'd thought of that himself. "Good idea, Constable. The rest of the servants aren't back yet, so you'd best station a man here in the hall to keep an eye on things. Put another man out front as well. I'll be back tomorrow morning." He reached for his hat. "Oh, and as the rest of the servants come in this evening, make sure you take their statements."

"Right, sir," Barnes held open the front door for the inspector. "Any ideas, sir?"

Witherspoon paused. He thought longingly of his former job in the records room at the Yard and wished he were back there. Yet it would never do to let on—everyone, including he himself was amazed by his apparently phenomenal powers of detection.

He gave Barnes a knowing smile. "Lots of ideas, Constable. But then, any fool can have ideas. I don't believe in ideas; I believe in facts."

"Absolutely, sir," Barnes quickly agreed.

"A rigourous and logical examination of the evidence, Constable, that's what will lead us to the truth. Let's not jump the gun here. No, no, that would never do. If I've said it once, I've said it a hundred times. Ideas are useless unless they're correct."

Mrs. Jeffries walked briskly down the back stairs of the big house in Upper Edmonton Gardens and into the warmth of the kitchen. She paused by the doorway and smiled as she surveyed her cozy kingdom. Betsy, the housemaid, was sitting at the long trestle table, polishing a tray of silver. Mrs. Goodge, the cook, was pulling a pan of bread out of the oven, and Wiggins, the footman, was standing in front of the cupboard. His hands were raised to his face, and he was poking himself in the cheeks.

"Wiggins, what are you doing?" Mrs. Jeffries asked. "This is the third time today I've seen you standing in front of a glass with your fingers boring into your face."

Betsy giggled. Mrs. Goodge snorted. Wiggins dropped his hands and whirled to face her. "Uh, I was a . . . a . . . ," he stammered.

"He's tryin to poke dimples into his cheeks," Betsy volunteered. "Wiggins is sweet on the new housemaid from down the road. But she told 'im she only likes a feller with dimples. Our Wiggins thinks if he keeps on poking 'imself long enough, he'll sprout a couple."

Mrs. Jeffries rolled her eyes. "Wiggins, that is nonsense. One is either born with dimples or one isn't. No amount of prodding at your flesh is going to produce them. Now look at you," she advanced on the hapless youth, "you've got two huge red scratches on your face. Go put a cool cloth on it before you get infection."

"But I've got the beginnings of 'em," Wiggins protested, "and look 'ere." He picked up a copy of one of Inspector Witherspoon's monthly magazines and thrust it toward the housekeeper. "See, look at this picture 'ere. That African's got ears as big as saucers and 'e wundn't born with 'em. He grew 'em, says so right 'ere."

"Wiggins," said Mrs. Jeffries patiently. "It is possible to distort one's flesh. But obviously you didn't read the article that accompanied the picture. If you had, you'd know that Africans begin changing the contours of their flesh in very early childhood. They certainly don't wait until your advanced age."

Wiggins was nineteen.

"But it's workin'. Look, one's starting right here." He pointed to his right cheek.

Mrs. Jeffries ran out of patience. She wasn't going to stand by and let the silly boy mutilate his face because of his latest infatuation, one of many, with a pretty housemaid.

"Don't be ridiculous. Pretty is as pretty does. Any young woman who is more concerned with a man's dimples than a man's character has about as much sense as Lady Afton's cocker spaniel."

Wiggins gasped. Lady Afton's spaniel was notorious. The animal was so stupid it didn't even recognize its mistress. "But, Mrs. Jeffries," the boy said, imploringly, "I really like this un."

"Wiggins, you like them all. Take my word for it, a young man as fine as yourself won't have to settle for an empty-headed little chit like that. You can do better."

"Will dinner be served at the usual time?" Mrs. Goodge interjected. She finished smearing butter on the top of the loaves and moved to the table.

"I'm not sure." Mrs. Jeffries frowned as she noticed the cook limping slightly. "Just keep the inspector's dinner in the oven. He's usually home by now. Is your rheumatism acting up, Mrs. Goodge?"

"Only a bit." The cook heaved herself into a chair.

"Leave the food on the stove and let the staff serve themselves for dinner. If your ankles are hurting, you need to stay off them. After dinner I'll make you a poultice."

"Much obliged."

Mrs. Jeffries cocked her head as footsteps sounded on the pavement outside the kitchen window. "There's the inspector now," she announced, bustling toward the stove. "You rest those ankles, Mrs. Goodge. I'll take his dinner up."

Witherspoon was sitting at the dining table when Mrs. Jeffries brought the tray in. She paused in the doorway and studied her employer. He was a tall, robust man with thinning dark brown hair and a neatly trimmed mustache. He had a long, rather angular face, a sharp, pointed nose and clear blue-gray eyes. He was staring dejectedly at the white lace tablecloth.

She knew what was wrong. She'd seen the signs before. Poor Inspector Witherspoon had been given another baffling case. Mrs. Jeffries's spirits soared.

"Good evening, Inspector," she said cheerfully. She sat the tray on the sideboard, picked up his plate and placed it in front of him. He immediately brightened up.

"Good evening, Mrs. Jeffries. How are things here at Upper Edmonton Gardens?"

It was an evocative question, one he asked when he was desperate for her to ask him how things were at the Yard—a kind of code they used for nosing into each other's business without actually having to come right out and pry.

"The household is running smoothly," she replied, picking up a cup of tea from the tray she'd brought up and taking the chair next to him. At Witherspoon's insistence, it was her habit to keep the Inspector company for his evening meal. "How are things at the Yard?"

"Not so good, I'm afraid," he sighed. "Crime. The criminal element. There's never any rest for those of us in the service of justice." He took a quick bite of roast beef and chewed hungrily.

Mrs. Jeffries waited patiently.

"Why, just today a highly respected doctor was found dead in his surgery. It could be murder. I tell you, Mrs. Jeffries, I don't know what this world is coming to. Everywhere you look—sin, immorality, vice, lascivious living."

Mrs. Jeffries privately thought these things weren't any better or worse than they had ever been. To her way of thinking, human nature was the one constant in an ever-changing world. But she contented herself with muttering a platitude as Witherspoon rambled on about the wickedness of modern life.

She was thinking about murder.

"Which doctor was it?" she finally asked.

The inspector was well into his lecture on immorality, so it took a few moments for him to realize what she was asking him. "Dr. Bartholomew Slocum. He had a practise in Knightsbridge."

"How was the doctor murdered?" Mrs. Jeffries asked softly.

"He may have been poisoned, but I'm not sure one can positively say the man was murdered. A vial of Syrup of Ipecac was found in his hand." Witherspoon shook his head. "But no, that still doesn't prove Dr. Slocum was deliberately murdered, despite the learned doctor's opinion."

"But I thought you said the doctor was dead?"

"Dr. Slocum is dead. It was Dr. Hightower, the man who happened to find the body, who hinted of murder. He's the one that notified us. It's pretty obvious to me that Hightower suspects foul play. I mean, why call the constable unless you think something is amiss? But until I get confirmation from our police surgeon, I'm not jumping to any conclusions."

"So you suspect the death might have been accidental?"

"I hope so," Witherspoon replied fervently. He looked at the kindly face of his housekeeper and said hopefully, "It could have been, couldn't it?"

"Of course." Mrs. Jeffries smiled gently. "I'm sure you're absolutely right, Inspector. It was probably accidental. Mind you, you'd think with him being a trained physician he'd be very careful when handling poison. But, I suppose any of us could get careless."

"Hmmm . . ." Witherspoon's face fell. "I hadn't really considered that," he mumbled. "He would be trained properly. And from the appearance of his surgery, one gets the impression he was a most careful man."

Wisely, Mrs. Jeffries let him finish his dinner before asking him any more questions. It was easier to wheedle information out of the inspector when his stomach was full.

"I'll have to interview the rest of the servants tomorrow," the inspector commented morosely. He hated questioning people. He could never tell whether or not someone was actually lying to him, and he knew, shocking as it was, that there were some people who lied to the police on a regular basis.

He glanced at Mrs. Jeffries. She smiled serenely, as though she thought him capable of moving mountains. The sight bolstered his resolve. Of course he could solve this case, if indeed, there was a case to be solved. Wasn't she always telling him how brilliant he was? Hadn't he solved several "unsolvable" crimes before? He stiffened his spine and smiled happily. He didn't know what had gotten into him today; of course he could do it.

Mrs. Jeffries rose to her feet and picked up the inspector's plate. "Well, of course, sudden death is always upsetting, not to mention suspicious."

"Just so," the inspector agreed. "Yet, frankly, I can't think why anyone would want to murder Dr. Slocum. He appears to be a highly respected and presumably very able medical man, so it's unlikely to have been a disgruntled patient. His butler didn't accuse him of drunkenness or gambling, and he didn't appear to need money." Witherspoon shrugged his shoulders. "So who would want to murder him? No, I'm beginning to think we'll find his death was an accident after all."

"I shouldn't be surprised if you're absolutely correct, as usual," Mrs. Jeffries said cheerfully. "Of course, my late husband always said that a sterling character and a fine reputation did not exempt one from the sins of another. As a matter of fact, he often said the best of men had the worst of enemies."

"Uh, yes, well, he would have been one to know," Witherspoon mused thoughtfully. Mrs. Jeffries's late husband had been a policeman in Yorkshire for over twenty years. Yet the inspector still wasn't sure what his housekeeper was on about. "Er, what did he mean by that?"

"It's quite simple, really. A good man, or woman, could easily make quite ruthless enemies by refusing to lie, or cheat or steal or cover up for wrongdoing, or—" She broke off and smiled. "Why, Inspector, you were teasing me. You knew precisely what I meant."

Witherspoon hadn't been joking, but he wasn't about to let her realize that. "Forgive me, Mrs. Jeffries," he replied, giving her the world-weary and wise smile he often got from his chief inspector. "I apologize for letting my sense of humor overcome my sense of decorum. As you know, I have the very highest regard for your late husband's accomplishments as a policeman."

"No apology is needed," she answered briskly. "When will you know for sure?"

His wise smile evaporated. He stared at her in confusion. "Know what?"

"Whether or not Dr. Slocum was poisoned."

"Ah, that. Yes, I'm hoping the police surgeon will have a report for me tomorrow."

She nodded. "I suppose that will determine whether the gentleman was actually poisoned. But if he was poisoned, how will you find out if it was deliberate or accidental?"

Witherspoon's face fell. Mrs. Jeffries immediately said, "Oh please don't answer that; it's such a silly question. Naturally you'll be able to determine whether or not it was murder by your investigation."

Betsy came in carrying a tray. "Your coffee, sir," she announced. She placed the tray on the sideboard and poured a cup for the inspector. As she turned to go, Mrs. Jeffries stopped her. "Betsy, is Smythe in the kitchen?"

"He's just got back from Howard's," Betsy answered, referring to the stables where the Witherspoon coach and horses were kept. Not that the inspector used them often, but he'd inherited the coach, horses and Smythe from a distant relative, and even though it cost a king's ransom to keep them in the city (hansoms were really so much more convenient), he hadn't the heart to sell them off.

Mrs. Jeffries smiled apologetically at the inspector and followed Betsy. "I must have a word with Smythe before he goes out."

Smythe was sitting at the table, his sleeves rolled up his forearms and his powerful frame hunched over a heaping plate of beef and potatoes, when Mrs. Jeffries came down the stairs. He started to get to his feet.

"Please, don't get up," she said quickly, motioning him back into his chair. "I just needed a quick word with you before you went out. I presume you are going to your usual place tonight?" She gave him a guileless smile.

"Ain't missed a night in seven years, have I?" Smythe said, watching her curiously. She sat down opposite him and glanced quickly around to make sure they weren't being overheard.

When she turned to face him, her eyes were sparkling and her chin was cocked at the determined angle he'd come to know well.

She was up to something, he thought. A right good snoop probably. Smythe's pulse picked up. He loved it when Mrs. J started her poking and prying. Livened things up considerably, it did. He leaned across the table and gave her a conspiratorial grin. "All right, Mrs. J. What you want me to do this time?"

CHAPTER 2

———————

Mrs. Jeffries was less startled by Smythe's statement than she was by the knowing expression on his face. Why, the man looked positively smug.

"*What do you want me to do this time?*" His words echoed in her mind. But surely he didn't realize what she was up to. She'd been so careful to be discreet in her investigations on the inspector's behalf. She always took great care to sound exceedingly casual when she sent Smythe off to find a bit of information on one of Witherspoon's cases. She'd deliberately couched her various requests in the most inconsequential language, as though they were things one did as a matter of course. Things to keep one busy and add a bit of color to one's life.

But perhaps she hadn't been quite as discreet as she'd thought, or perhaps the other servants at Upper Edmonton Gardens were a good deal quicker off the mark than she'd realized. Keeping her placid smile firmly in place, she studied Smythe, trying to get a clue as to how much he had guessed about her activities.

Smythe was a tall, dark-haired, powerfully built man with a face that some would call brutish unless they took the time to notice his kind brown eyes. Mrs. Jeffries sighed softly, suspecting that those eyes saw a great deal more than she'd ever guessed and that the rest of the household, save for the inspector, knew precisely what she was doing. They weren't fools.

Oh well, she told herself firmly, it can't be helped. Besides, her little investigations certainly made their lives more interesting.

"It's more a matter of what I want you to not do," Mrs. Jeffries finally replied.

He stared at her quizzically. "Come again, Mrs. J?"

"I don't want you to go to your usual tonight, Smythe. Wouldn't you like to try a new place? Perhaps one of the pubs in Knightsbridge?"

"Knightsbridge?" He regarded her thoughtfully. "I'm right fond of the ale they serve down at the Blue Boar, but seein' as how it's for you, all right."

"Thank you, Smythe." Mrs. Jeffries smiled gratefully and leaned closer to the coachman. "Now. You might have to try several places, but I want you to find out everything you can about a man named Dr. Bartholomew Slocum."

"What's he done?" Smythe took another bite of roast beef.

"Nothing. He's dead."

Smythe's eyebrows shot up, but he kept silent.

"He might have been murdered," she continued.

"*Might* have been murdered," Smythe repeated. "Can't the police tell for sure?"

"He may have been poisoned," she explained, "but the police won't know for certain until after the postmortem. Inspector Witherspoon should have the surgeon's report by tomorrow."

"Then why do you want me to go out snoopin' tonight?" he asked. "In't that puttin' the cart before the horse?"

"Let's just say this is in the nature of a reconnaissance expedition," she replied. "Besides, I've got a feeling about this case. Don't you want to go to Knightsbridge?"

"I don't mind," he said, shrugging one massive shoulder and giving her a cocky grin. "I always fancied myself a bit of a scout, sneaking off into enemy territory, pokin' about and seein' what I can . . ."

"Good," she interrupted firmly, knowing Smythe's tendency to get carried away. "Dr. Slocum's surgery is on Barret Street. See if you can find any of the servants from his household and find out as much as you can."

"Anything in particular you want to know?"

Mrs. Jeffries frowned as she thought back over everything Witherspoon had told her. He hadn't been very specific. She made a mental note to remedy that situation. But the inspector had said the man might have been poisoned.

"Find out what the household had eaten that day, if you can," she said, "and, of course, anything else."

"Right." Smythe rose to his feet. "I'd best be off then." He headed for the door.

As his hand reached for the knob, Mrs. Jeffries called out. "Smythe."

He half turned and gazed at her curiously.

"You will, of course, be very careful," she said softly, her expression concerned.

"Don't fret, Mrs. J," he replied, grabbing the knob and pulling the door open. "I'm always careful."

Mrs. Jeffries fervently hoped so.

"I do wish you'd eat breakfast with me," Witherspoon said as Mrs. Jeffries poured herself a cup of tea and sat down next to him.

"I had my breakfast hours ago, and it really wouldn't be proper for me to eat formal meals with you, Inspector." She smiled. "You know that."

"I don't believe it would be all that scandalous. With all due respect to Her Majesty, this isn't Buckingham Palace. You are my housekeeper, and it's not as if we're particularly formal here." He sighed, rather dramatically. "Eating every meal by oneself gets a tad lonely, you know."

"But you're not alone," she assured him. "I'm sitting right here keeping you company. Furthermore, if you were *married,* you'd have a wife to eat your meals with." She looked at him expectantly.

Witherspoon shook his head and shoved another forkful of fried egg into his mouth. Mrs. Jeffries gazed at him thoughtfully while he finished his breakfast. She so wished the inspector would find a nice young lady. The dear man was lonely. The fact that a wife might very well inhibit her own passion for investigating didn't concern her in the least.

"You know my work is far too dangerous for me to take on the responsibility of a wife," Witherspoon said. "Why, anything could happen to me. I spend my life investigating heinous crimes, murders . . . I can't risk it. I've got so many enemies."

Mrs. Jeffries refrained from commenting that until rather recently the inspector had spent most of his life in the records room at Scotland Yard. She knew why he wasn't married, why the very idea terrified him. Witherspoon was notoriously shy when it came to women. She decided to try another tactic.

"Really, Inspector," she began earnestly, "you know very well that a man of your intelligence is always half a dozen steps ahead of any criminal that might be lurking about."

The inspector beamed.

"Certainly your work is dangerous," she continued, "but there are many men who have even more frightful occupations, and they have the comfort of wives and children."

Turning a bright pink, Witherspoon lowered his fork and gazed fondly at his housekeeper. The dear woman was always looking out for him. But on this subject, he really rather wished she wouldn't press him. "Mrs. Jeffries."

"Yes," she replied, giving him an innocent smile.

The words lodged in his throat as he gazed at her. He remembered all too well how different his life had been before her arrival. But then so much had been different— he'd been nothing more than a records clerk when his Aunt Euphemia died and everything changed. Before he'd had time to catch his breath, he'd inherited a house, a fortune,

Smythe and Wiggins. (Well, he hadn't actually inherited them, but as they'd worked for his Aunt Euphemia and she'd been the one to leave him her entire fortune, he could hardly turn them out.)

Yet his life hadn't really changed until he'd taken up residence here eighteen months ago—which had necessitated hiring a housekeeper. Mrs. Jeffries.

Witherspoon frowned as he realized it was soon after that that he'd discovered his amazing abilities as a detective.

"Inspector," Mrs. Jeffries said softly, seeing that the man was daydreaming again, "there's an absolutely lovely woman staying at Lady Afton's. A Miss Liza Cannonberry. Lady Afton has the very highest regard for you, and I'm sure she'd be happy to arrange an introduction."

"Eh?" Witherspoon blinked, but he had heard Mrs. Jeffries's last few words. "Arrange an introduction," he repeated hastily, trying not to panic. "Oh no, I don't think that would do at all."

Luckily for him, the door opened and Betsy came in. Mrs. Jeffries frowned ever so slightly when she recognized the man following behind the maid. Rising quickly to her feet, she forced a polite smile to her lips.

"Inspector Nivens," she said smoothly. "How very nice to see you. Would you care for some breakfast?"

She sincerely hoped he wouldn't. Of all the people she'd ever met, one of the few she'd disliked on sight was Inspector Nigel Nivens. Further acquaintance with the man hadn't changed her opinion either.

Nivens was a slender man of slightly more than average height with a ferretlike face, slicked back dull blond hair and the coldest gray eyes she'd ever seen. As he crossed the room, she noticed how his gaze swept the table, taking in her empty teacup sitting next to Witherspoon's breakfast dishes.

"Thank you, but no. I had breakfast early, I was at the Yard by seven." Nivens gave her a cool, superior smile before turning his attention to Inspector Witherspoon.

"My goodness, you're an eager fellow," Witherspoon

said cheerfully. "Did you hear that, Mrs. Jeffries? Inspector Nivens has been up and working since the crack of dawn."

"How very conscientious of you," she murmured, knowing full well that Nivens's sly dig had sailed completely over Witherspoon's head.

"Would you like a cup of tea, then?" Witherspoon asked.

Mrs. Jeffries stiffened. She hoped Nivens would have the good grace to refuse and be off about his business.

The odious man had made it clear on numerous occasions that he didn't believe for one minute that Gerald Witherspoon was much of a detective. He'd actually had the gall after those notorious Kensington High Street murders to tell the chief inspector that Witherspoon's success in apprehending the murderer had been sheer luck. Either that, or he'd had help.

Inspector Nivens made Mrs. Jeffries very, very nervous.

"I'm afraid I don't have time," Nivens replied, straightening his spine pompously. "There's been a robbery in Holland Park. I'm on my way there now. But as I had to pass by your street, I thought I'd bring this to you." He pulled an envelope from his coat pocket and laid it on the table. "It's the surgeon's report on that Knightsbridge matter."

"Why, that's jolly decent of you."

"It was no trouble." He turned and glanced at Mrs. Jeffries. "Of course, I knew you'd want to see this right away."

Mrs. Jeffries stopped herself from looking at the envelope. Her hands itched to pick it up and tear it open. But she knew that would never do. Nivens would like nothing more than to catch her meddling in the inspector's cases. But Hepzibah Jeffries hadn't lived fifty-seven years on God's green earth without learning a few tricks.

Witherspoon used his breakfast knife to slit open the flap. Mrs. Jeffries would have bet two weeks' housekeeping money that that wasn't the first time this morning that seal had been broken. But naturally, one couldn't say anything.

"I'd best be on my way," Nivens said cheerfully, watching Inspector Witherspoon fumbling around to pull the report out.

"I'll see you to the door," Mrs. Jeffries murmured politely. She followed him out of the dining room and down the hall. As they reached the front door, Nivens turned and smiled slyly.

"This might be a difficult case for the inspector," he said softly. "Poisonings always are. Wouldn't you agree?"

"Actually, I'd have no idea," she said innocently. "And neither would Inspector Witherspoon until after he'd read the surgeon's report."

He flushed a deep red as he realized his mistake. But he recovered quicker than she'd hoped.

"You're a very clever woman, Mrs. Jeffries," he said smoothly. "The inspector is lucky to have you in his employment."

"Oh no, Inspector Nivens," she assured him. "It is I who am fortunate. Not everyone is privileged to work for such a kind and brilliant man as Gerald Witherspoon."

Nivens's eyes narrowed slightly as they gazed at each other in silence. From the drawing room, the clock chimed the hour.

"It's getting late," he finally said. "Must be off. Good day to you, madam."

"Good day, Inspector."

As the door closed behind him, she leaned against the wood and took a few seconds to compose herself. Dealing with Nigel Nivens always had the effect of putting her in a foul mood.

Straightening, she patted the pocket of her skirt and then smiled in satisfaction as she hurried back to the dining room.

She found Witherspoon holding the surgeon's report at arm's length and squinting at the handwriting.

"Mrs. Jeffries," he grumbled, "I can't see a ruddy thing.

Do you know where my spectacles are?" He glanced up at her. "It's not that I really need them," he explained, "but the light isn't very good in here and this writing is dreadfully small. I don't know why they can't teach these medical chaps decent penmanship."

"I'm so sorry, Inspector. I have no idea where they are." She sent up a quick, silent prayer for forgiveness as she told the fib. "Would you like me to read the report to you?"

Witherspoon turned quickly to glance at the clock on the sideboard and saw that it had gone eight. "It is getting late, and I do need to know the surgeon's findings before I go back to Knightsbridge. I mean, there's not much point in going back at all if we find the chap had a stroke or something." He handed her the report. "Thank you, Mrs. Jeffries. That's most kind of you to offer."

It took less than five minutes to read, and at the end, both of them were shaking their heads.

"Mushrooms," exclaimed Witherspoon. "I've never heard of such a thing. And in the man's soup! Gracious. Dreadful business," he mumbled. "Absolutely dreadful."

"Some mushrooms are quite poisonous," Mrs. Jeffries said slowly. "According to the surgeon, the mushroom Dr. Slocum ingested was called '*amanite phalloide*'—I think that's what we used to call the death cap. Oh yes, Inspector, those are quite deadly." She frowned slightly as something tugged at the back of her mind.

"Apparently so. Oh well," he said cheerfully, "at least I had the foresight to send Dr. Slocum's luncheon dishes to the Yard for examination. No doubt that'll make the Home Office happy."

"I beg your pardon? What does the Home Office have to do with Dr. Slocum's lunch dishes?"

"Why, everything. Thanks to my quick action, the police surgeon didn't have to do much cutting on the body. It says so in the report; they spotted part of a poison mushroom at the bottom of the soup bowl right away. Most convenient for the surgeon." He leaned toward her and lowered his voice. "Her Majesty doesn't really approve, you know."

Mystified, she stared at him. "Approve of what?"

"Cutting on people. She's not all that keen on the surgeons mucking about with someone's body. The Home Office is far happier when we can spot the cause of death without having to actually do any cutting. Just between you and me and the clock on the sideboard, I'd bet my next hot dinner that once our medical man spotted that mushroom, he didn't do any cutting at all. None of them like to upset the Home Office."

"I see." Mrs. Jeffries glanced down at the report in her lap. No doubt, the inspector was right. But really, not wanting to upset the Home Office seemed an awfully useless excuse for not doing one's job properly.

Witherspoon nodded. "Now the doctor is hardly likely to have gone out and plucked a poisonous mushroom from out beneath a bush and popped it into his soup, is he? So I suppose my next step is to find out how it got there."

"That's true."

"Perhaps it was accidental?" He brightened at the thought. "Yes, I expect that's it. A poisonous mushroom accidentally got mixed into a batch of edible ones and ended up in Dr. Slocum's stomach."

"That's possible." Mrs. Jeffries laid the report next to Witherspoon's plate and gave him a serene smile. "And I'm sure you'll find out precisely what happened."

Witherspoon smiled and sincerely hoped his housekeeper was right.

"Oh leave off, Wiggins," Betsy teased. "We all know why you're so keen to wash the fence." Both she and Mrs. Goodge laughed as the boy turned a bright red.

"I'm not *keen* to wash the bloomin' thing," he protested, reaching for another bun and glancing furtively at the housekeeper. "But it's my job, now, in't it, and Mrs. Jeffries wants it done."

Mrs. Jeffries was only half-listening. Her mind was on the

information she'd wheedled out of Inspector Witherspoon about the late Dr. Slocum. She was thinking about the physical description of the victim's face that the inspector had given her as he was putting on his coat. Something about it disturbed her, but she couldn't quite put her finger on it.

"Get on with you," Betsy chided. "Who do you think you're foolin'? You just want to hang out in front so you can moon over that Miss Cannonberry who's staying at Lady Afton's. You're awfully fickle, Wiggins. Yesterday you were in love with that housemaid down the road, but the minute you laid eyes on Miss Cannonberry, you forgot her quick enough. Admit it, you want to be outside there when they walks that dumb dog."

"That's not true," he protested around a mouthful of bun. "And what about you? You hotfoot it outside quick enough whenever that Constable Griffith's around."

"Ohhh . . ." Betsy gasped indignantly and drew a sharp breath. "Of all the rotten—"

Mrs. Jeffries decided it was time to intervene. "Now, now, you two. That's enough. Stop teasing each other. All it ever does is hurt feelings." The two combatants glowered at each other but kept silent.

The housekeeper rose to her feet. "Tea break's over," she announced briskly. "Betsy, you go finish dusting the drawing room, and Wiggins, if you're going to clean the fence, get on with it."

"I think I'll go have a rest," Mrs. Goodge said, rising stiffly to her feet.

As soon as the kitchen was empty, Mrs. Jeffries glanced at the clock and frowned. Where on earth could Smythe be? Mrs. Goodge said he hadn't come in for breakfast, and neither Betsy nor Wiggins had seen hide nor hair of him this morning.

She began putting the cups on the tray, telling herself he was probably already at Howard's, polishing a harness or exercising the horses.

The kitchen door opened and she whirled around.

"Good gracious, you look awful," she exclaimed, looking at the pale-faced Smythe as he slumped against the door-frame. "Are you ill?"

"It's a bleedin' wonder I'm not dead," he muttered, moving carefully toward the table. "Is there any tea left?"

"What happened?" Mrs. Jeffries asked in alarm. This certainly wasn't the first time she'd seen Smythe looking the worse for wear, especially after a night of pub crawling. But today he looked particularly greenish around the gills. She hurried across to the stove as Smythe stumbled toward the table. Snatching a mug off the wooden drain board, she poured it full of strong, hot tea.

"Gracious, Smythe," she said, plonking the mug next to him. "You look ghastly."

He groaned. "Not so loud, please. Me head feels like they's a team of horses kicking me brains in." He took a long drink, his eyes rolling toward the ceiling as the hot liquid poured down his throat.

"I tell ya, Mrs. J," he said after he'd gulped the entire mugful, "it's no wonder I look like the back end of a cow after what I had to drink last night. The swill they serve in some of those Knightsbridge pubs could choke a pig."

"I'm so sorry, Smythe." Mrs. Jeffries sighed. "I had no idea you'd end up like this when I sent you out." Feeling guilty, she gazed at him sympathetically. "Is there anything I can do?"

"Another cuppa would help." He held the mug out, and she quickly got to her feet and poured him more tea.

"Don't fret so," he continued. "I don't mind makin' a sacrifice for you," he paused and looked her directly in the eyes before adding, "and the inspector."

Mrs. Jeffries knew that he meant what he said. If Inspector Witherspoon hadn't kept both Smythe and Wiggins in his employ, both men would be in dire straits. Wiggins was no more a trained footman than she was the Queen of Sheba, and Smythe, for all his strength and intelligence, would be desolate without Bow and Arrow, the inspector's horses.

Mrs. Jeffries waited patiently while the coachman finished his tea. After he'd drained the mug, he sat back and gave her a cocky grin.

"Were you successful with your inquiries?" she asked.

Smythe nodded. "I found one of the footmen. Not much of a talker at first."

"Oh dear," she said, clearly disappointed. "You mean you didn't get anything out of him?"

"Course I did. Once the feller had a few pints down his gullet, his tongue loosened considerably," the coachman replied. "It seems the good doctor wasn't liked very much by his staff. According to the footman, he was a right ol' tartar."

"He didn't treat them very well?" Mrs. Jeffries said, wondering if that could possibly be a motive for murder. Then she realized it probably wasn't. If servants habitually killed harsh employers, half the gentry would be dead and buried.

"Treated 'em rotten, but he paid 'em good. That's what the footman claimed. Said the only reason the servants put up with the man was because he paid better than most."

"Were you able to find out what they'd had to eat that day?"

"They had porridge and tea for breakfast, not like here, where we get a decent meal of bacon and eggs. Then at lunch they had soup and bread with cheese. When they's all arrived back, the police were there, so they didn't get much for dinner that night." Smythe grinned. "The footman was real niggled about that too, said it wun't right, just because the man was dead shouldna mean the rest of them need starve. But the cook was wailin' and cryin' and not about to stir herself to fix 'em a bite o' supper."

"Did he say what kind of soup they'd eaten?"

"Mushroom." He paused as he saw Mrs. Jeffries eyes widen. "Is that important?"

"It could be," she replied thoughtfully. "Did the doctor eat the same meal?"

"No. He had the soup and cheese, all right, but he had himself a couple of lamb chops too. And a bottle of wine. Seems Dr. Slocum was right fond of the stuff. The footman claimed he sloughed it back like water every time he sat down to a meal."

"I see," she murmured. But if the doctor had been poisoned by the soup, why hadn't the rest of the household died?

"You want me to go back tonight? See what else I can find out?"

Mrs. Jeffries grappled with her conscience for all of two seconds and then gave the coachman a grateful smile. "If you wouldn't mind, Smythe. You might be able to learn something more. Something we can use to help the inspector solve this case."

It was pointless to pretend any longer that Smythe didn't know what she was up to.

"Are you going out then?" Betsy tossed a blond curl off her shoulder and watched as Mrs. Jeffries put on her hat.

"Yes, I'm going over to Bond Street to try and match that material for the dining-room curtains." The housekeeper could hardly announce that she was really going to Dr. Slocum's to search the scene of the crime. Or could she?

She paused, still holding her hatpin. "No, that's not true."

Since her talk with Smythe, Mrs. Jeffries thought it best to clear the air. The other servants had probably guessed the truth too, and it was best to make a clean breast of things. Truth to tell, her conscience was bothering her.

"It's not?" Betsy stared at her curiously.

"Come sit down, please. There's something I need to tell you."

Obediently, Betsy laid down her dust cloth and crossed the room to the settee. Mrs. Jeffries patted the spot beside her, and the girl sat down.

Mrs. Jeffries took a deep breath. "I'm sure you've guessed that occasionally, well . . . I, that is, we, do a few minor things to help the inspector with his cases."

Betsy nodded vigorously. "Oh yes, like that time during them 'orrible Kensington High Street murders when you 'ad me goin' round to talk to all the shop assistants. Or when you send Wiggins out with notes and all, or hide the inspector's spectacles so you can read the police surgeon's report, like this morning."

"Goodness, you saw that?" Mrs. Jeffries was shocked. She hadn't realized she'd been that indiscreet.

"Oh yes. It's like when you're on to something about one of the inspector's cases and you send Smythe off to a pub or get Mrs. Goodge to start gossipin'. Though mind you, I don't see how Mrs. Goodge knows so much about everyone in London, seein' as 'ow she never leaves the kitchen."

Mrs. Jeffries's amazement turned to relief, and she laughed. "So you've known all along. Have the others caught on as well?"

Betsy laughed too. "Well, I wouldna say we've known right from the start. It took us a bit a time to work it all out. But we're all of the same mind. We think what you're doin' is right. Inspector Witherspoon is the kindest man that ever lived. He's been so good to all of us. We'll do anything we can for him. And with the likes of that awful Inspector Nivens always sniffin' around, I reckon our inspector needs all the help he can get."

"I'm glad you feel that way," Mrs. Jeffries said softly.

"He kept me from havin' to walk the streets," Betsy continued earnestly. "And he kept Smythe and Wiggins after his Aunt Euphemia died, when everyone knows he need a coachman and a footman about as much as I need a diamond tiara to do my dustin' in, not that I wouldn't like to 'ave one, mind you."

"So you and the rest of the staff don't mind doing a little, shall we say, detective work, for our dear inspector?"

"Mind? You must be pulling me leg. Course we don't mind. It's interestin', and it's little enough to do for the man after all he's done for us."

"Good. Then you won't mind taking charge of the house this morning while I go to Knightsbridge?"

Betsy shook her head. "What are you going to do there?"

"I'm going to search the scene of the crime." Mrs. Jeffries rose to her feet. "We need to make sure a clue hasn't been overlooked."

She walked out into the pale October sunshine. Wiggins was halfheartedly washing the black wrought-iron fence as he kept an eagle eye out for Miss Cannonberry.

She started down the steps and then paused as she realized it couldn't hurt any to learn as much as possible about mushrooms. Leaving Wiggins happily staring up the street, she turned swiftly, went back inside and into the inspector's study.

A few moments later she came out again, a folded note clutched in her hand. "Wiggins. Come here, please. I need you to run an errand for me."

The boy looked crestfallen. "Now? You want me to leave now? But, Mrs. Jeffries, I'm right in the middle of this."

"It'll still be here when you get back," she assured him.

Reluctantly, Wiggins dropped the washrag back into the pail and trudged over to the housekeeper. He stared at the note in her hand. "Where do you want me to go?"

"To Mudie's," she replied, referring to the circulating library. She handed Wiggins the note. "Give this to Mr. Oliphant, and then wait until he finds a book for you. Bring it back straight away and have Betsy put it in my room."

After he'd gone, Mrs. Jeffries hurried to the corner and turned toward Hyde Park. She decided to walk to Dr. Slocum's—she needed to think.

CHAPTER 3

Mrs. Jeffries stopped across the road and studied the tall yellow-brick house of the late Dr. Slocum. The paint on the front door and around the windows looked new, the earth in the tiny space behind the wrought-iron fence was freshly turned and planted with bulbs, the stone steps were swept clean and the brass plate with Dr. Slocum's name and surgery hours was polished to a dull sheen.

Mrs. Jeffries crossed the road and headed for the police constable standing to one side of the brass door knocker. She was relieved when she recognized Constable Barnes's familiar craggy face.

"Good morning, Constable," she said cheerfully. "Isn't it a beautiful day."

"Why it's Mrs. Jeffries. What are you doing here, ma'am?" Constable Barnes looked both delighted and puzzled.

"The most dreadful thing has happened, Constable," Mrs. Jeffries said, gesturing to the front door. "I really must get inside there. Inspector Witherspoon mislaid his cigar case yesterday, and he hasn't the faintest idea where!"

Courteously, Barnes had already reached for the doorknob when he remembered this was a murder scene. But before he could say anything, Mrs. Jeffries was brushing past him and sailing inside.

"And it's a most valuable case," she continued, giving

32

him a wide smile. "His father gave it to him for his twenty-first birthday. The poor man will be devastated if he's lost it."

"Can't he find it himself?" Barnes asked helplessly.

"I don't think so," she replied, moving briskly down the hall. "You know the inspector; he's far too involved in the case to remember a little detail like where he put his cigar case. But don't worry, I'll be very careful."

"I suppose it's all right, then," Barnes called out when he couldn't quite work up the nerve to stop the woman.

Mrs. Jeffries threw Barnes one last, confident smile as she reached the surgery and quickly stepped inside.

She didn't have much time and she knew it. Turning, she scanned the room, her observant eyes taking in as much as she could with one glance.

She moved to the row of cabinets, stopped by the first one and peered inside. Through the glass, she saw Dr. Slocum's medical instruments. In the cabinet next to that, she saw rows of neatly labeled medicines and chemicals.

Nothing odd here, she thought, turning toward the desk.

Cocking her head, she picked up one side of the large book that was lying open on it and read the title. *Adamson's Medical Comprehensive on Common Poisons and Antidotes.*

Surprised, she stared at the page and wondered how the inspector could have neglected to mention this to her. He probably forgot, she thought. She dropped the edge of the book and turned her attention to the desk. Searching quickly through the drawers, she found nothing out of the ordinary.

Nothing that gave her a clue as to why or who had murdered the doctor . . . if he'd been murdered. But she rather suspected he had, especially after seeing the open book on the desk. And hearing Smythe's report, Dr. Slocum had probably guessed he'd been poisoned as well.

But why? Why would a highly successful member of the British medical establishment think he'd been poisoned?

She could think of only one answer. Because he knew someone wanted him dead.

Dropping to her knees, she peered under the desk. Nothing there. She continued searching the floor, tugging her long skirt high to prevent it from slowing her pace. She noticed how clean everything, including the carpet, was.

Beneath the medicine cabinet nearest the door, she spotted a small dark object. She reached into the shadowy space and pulled it out.

Holding it up to the light, she saw that it was a small piece of cork, approximately the size of her little fingernail. Her brown eyes narrowed thoughtfully as she studied it. Then she looked again around the room, noting how there wasn't a speck of dust anywhere, not even in the corners. She stood up and ran her fingers over the top of the cabinet. Her hand stilled. Bending close, she saw a fine layer of particles, not quite dust and not quite grit, scattered in the center of the wood.

From the hall, Mrs. Jeffries heard the sound of footsteps. She straightened and smoothed her long skirt just as the door opened and Inspector Witherspoon appeared.

"Mrs. Jeffries," he said in surprise. "What on earth are you doing here?"

"Finding your cigar case," she replied, pulling the case out of her skirt pocket and handing it to him. "I realized this morning when I handed you your coat that it wasn't in the pocket. I thought you must have lost it when you were here yesterday."

"Gracious me," he exclaimed, taking the case and staring at it with a puzzled frown. "How very clever of you. I didn't even know it was missing."

"No, of course you didn't. Once you're on a case, Inspector, your mind is fully occupied."

Witherspoon smiled modestly. "Well, it's very good of you to come find this for me." His smile faded and the puzzled look came back into his eyes. "But how did you know I'd mislaid it here?"

"Now, now, Inspector, don't be so modest. Why, you know very well I used your own methods of deduction to find it."

"You did?"

"Naturally, one can't be around a mind such as yours for very long without picking up a trick or two." She laughed merrily. "You had it yesterday at lunch. Then you were called here. As I said, it wasn't in your coat pocket when I checked this morning, and it wasn't at home. Obviously I knew there was only one place it could be. Here."

"Why didn't you mention it to me before I left?" he asked. "There was no need to trouble yourself to come all this way—"

"It was no trouble at all," she assured him. "And I don't like to bother you with trifling matters like a missing cigar case when you're so very busy. Besides, I had to come to Knightsbridge anyway. There's a draper's shop on Brompton Road that can match the fabric in the dining-room curtains."

"Well, as long as it was no bother, thank you." Witherspoon sighed happily. He was such a lucky man— how many other housekeepers would go to so much effort to see to his every comfort and need? And he was most fond of his cigar case. Even though he rarely smoked. Tobacco made him ill.

"Do you know, it's the most curious thing," Mrs. Jeffries said.

"What is?"

"I found the case beneath this medicine cabinet. The corner was sticking out. It must have slipped out of your pocket when you were searching the room yesterday. But when I went to pick it up, I found this as well." She handed the piece of cork to him. "Isn't that odd?"

"Looks like a piece of cork," he muttered, squinting at it. "Wonder what it was doing there."

"Yes," she said thoughtfully, "I wondered the same thing myself. Strange, isn't it?"

"How so?"

"Well, this room. It's so clean, and I couldn't help but notice when I was looking for the case that there isn't a speck of dust anywhere. Except for right here." She pointed to the top of the cabinet.

"Hmmm . . ." Witherspoon frowned as he bent over and stared at the spot. "You're right. There's dust on top of the cabinet. But that's probably just a patch the cleaning woman missed."

"Really? Do you think so. In a doctor's surgery?" She shook her head. "I daresay the rest of the room has had a thorough cleaning; there's not even a speck of dirt in the corners. It's peculiar that the maid would miss this. And I'm not all that sure this is dust. Doesn't it look a bit too coarse?"

"Hmmm, yes, actually. It does."

"And, of course, this is a doctor's surgery. The maid would have to insure it wasn't just tidied up, but really cleaned every single day."

"Naturally, naturally," Witherspoon agreed absently. Suddenly his eyes lit up in understanding. "That would mean that, perhaps, if this room was cleaned the morning of Dr. Slocum's death, that this," he held up the piece of cork, "was dropped either by Slocum himself or . . . the murderer."

"Murderer?" she queried softly. "Then you think the victim's death was deliberate and not accidental?"

"I'm afraid so," he said with a sigh. "One of the constables found another poisonous mushroom in the cooling pantry. It was in a bowl with some edible ones, and it couldn't possibly have gotten there accidentally."

"Why not?" Mrs. Jeffries wasn't surprised to find out the doctor had been murdered, but she was a bit puzzled by this new piece of evidence.

"Because the other mushrooms, the edible ones, had been properly cleaned. The poisonous one hadn't. There was dirt on the cap and stem, as if it had just been pulled from the ground and tossed into the bowl." He broke off and stared at the piece of cork again and then walked over to the medicine cabinet, opened the door and pulled out a brown bottle. "Aha, just as I thought."

"What is it?"

"Why, this piece of cork. Look here." He held the bottle toward his housekeeper. "It was obviously dropped by the doctor himself. The top is made of cork." Bending down, he peered inside for a moment and then said, "Half the bottles and vials in here are topped with cork."

Mrs. Jeffries looked over his shoulder at the inside of the cabinet. She reached around him and drew out a dark blue vial. "Yes, but look here. These tops are made from much finer-grained cork, while that one," she pointed to the piece he was still holding, "is very coarse. I think it's from a much larger bottle than the ones Dr. Slocum has here in his medicine cabinet."

Witherspoon's face mirrored his disappointment. He hated clues that didn't make any sense. "Hmmm, yes. I see what you mean." Drat, he thought, now he'd have to try and figure out the significance of the piece of cork. If it had any significance. He didn't relish talking to the maid again, either. She'd told him she didn't much care for policemen.

Confident she'd set her inspector on the correct path of inquiry, Mrs. Jeffries straightened. "I must be off now. Will you be home at your normal time for dinner?"

"Yes," he murmured, still staring dejectedly at the small piece of inscrutable evidence. "After I speak with the maid, the constable and I are going house to house around the garden to see if anyone saw anything unusual yesterday."

"Fine, then. We'll expect you at six." She waved a cheerful good-bye and left.

Mrs. Jeffries left the inspector still standing morosely in the surgery. As soon as she was in the hall, she stopped, listening for sounds of activity within the household. But there was nothing but silence. The servants, no doubt, had taken to their rooms or gone out for the day.

She decided this might be a good opportunity to find out

how easy it was to get in and out of the Slocum house. Moving quietly, she went down the hall to the back stairs, past the door leading to the kitchen and out onto the tiny terrace that faced the garden. The first thing she must do was see if the garden gate was kept locked. But she hadn't taken two steps before she was stopped in her tracks.

"You there." The voice was flat, twangy and loud enough to wake the dead.

Mrs. Jeffries turned and saw a wrinkled, white-haired old woman wearing a bright red dress and hobbling toward her at surprising speed. "Were you addressing me, madam?" she asked politely.

"You're the only one out here," the woman replied and Mrs. Jeffries knew from her accent that she was an American.

"I'm Mrs. Archie Crookshank, first name's Luty Belle. Who're you?"

"Hepzibah Jeffries." She was trying to think of a plausible reason for being on Dr. Slocum's terrace, but she found she didn't have to. Mrs. Crookshank kept right on talking.

"Is the old geezer dead, then?" she continued. "I expect he was murdered, what with the constable swarming all over the place. That's not surprising. He wasn't exactly well liked around these parts." She broke off and cackled. "Shouldn't speak ill of dead, I suppose, but land's sake, that man could set a saint to running in the opposite direction." She peered at Mrs. Jeffries suspiciously, her brown eyes narrowing. "You ain't any kin of his, are you?"

"No." She smiled. "I didn't know the deceased. I'm merely here because my employer happens to have business in the house. But why do you think he was mur—"

"Good," Luty Crookshank interrupted, "then I ain't offendin' none." She raised a wrinkled hand and pointed to the house next door. "I live right there. Fancy place, ain't it? But Archie, that's my late husband, he was English, and after he'd made his fortune in the mines back in Colorado, he was determined to come back here. Been here now nigh onto twenty years. Ain't surprised someone finally killed ol' Slocum. He was the kind that always comes to a bad end."

"Did you know Dr. Slocum well, Mrs. Crookshank?" Mrs. Jeffries asked.

"Call me Luty Belle. Yup, I knew him pretty good. Didn't like him much. Too sly for my blood. Always pussyfootin' around trying to butter people up and then slippin' off and trying to listen in to private talks. Why, just last Saturday, when I was havin' my tea party, Slocum practically hid behind a bush so he could hear what Dr. Hightower and Mrs. Leslie were jawin' about."

"You mean the man was eavesdropping?"

Luty Belle snorted. "He did it all the time. I almost didn't invite him, but, well . . . he was a neighbor." She broke off and frowned. "Hey, you there, boy," she bellowed.

Mrs. Jeffries looked up in time to see a young gardener come out from behind a tree. Grinning, he waved and then hurried across the garden toward them.

"Mornin', Garret," Luty Belle shouted. "Did you dig them dead eyes out yet?"

The gardener shook his head. "No, ma'am."

"What are you waiting for, boy?" she said indignantly. "I told you, them things are poisonous. Now, you get over there and get to it."

"What things?" Mrs. Jeffries wasn't above interrupting herself.

"Dead eyes. Mushrooms."

"But, Mrs. Crookshank," the gardener said earnestly, "I can't dig them out. They're gone."

"Gone! What are you talkin' about? They didn't just get up and go for a stroll. There was a whole danged nest of them under that tree. Mrs. Leslie couldn't finish eatin' her cake after she found out what they was. Now, you go have another look, boy, and if'n you find 'em, I'll give you a guinea—"

"Luty Belle," Mrs. Jeffries shouted, and both of them turned to stare at her. "Forgive me, please. But this is very important."

"What is?" Luty Belle asked with a glare.

"Are you saying that during your tea party, which I presume was last Saturday, you saw some poison mushrooms?"

"Yes, there was a whole slew of them, right under that big tree out there where I was having my party. As soon as I saw they was dead eyes, I yelled at Garret here to dig 'em out as soon as he could." Luty Belle cocked her head to one side and stared hard at Mrs. Jeffries. "Why are you so interested?"

She debated about telling the truth and finally decided she had no choice. "Because Dr. Slocum was killed by eating a poison mushroom. Tell me, Luty Belle, did you mention the mushrooms during the party?"

She nodded slowly, her expression somber. "'Fraid so. Everybody heard me."

"Who is everybody?"

"Let's see, Dr. Slocum was here and Colonel Seaward, he's the gentleman that lives in that mausoleum at the end of the garden." She pointed to her left. "Mrs. Leslie was here and Dr. Hightower. The Wakeman sisters were both here— no, they'd already left by then because they was fixin' to go to visit their niece in Shropshire and had to catch a train. Let me see, who else? The Baxters had gone by then too, but Mr. and Mrs. Eversole were still eating . . . Course, they never leave until the last crumb's gone, not that I mind. That's what it's for—"

"I think, Luty Belle," Mrs. Jeffries interrupted softly, "you'd better talk to my employer." She turned to the boy. "Could you please go inside and ask to see Inspector Witherspoon? Tell him Mrs. Crookshank needs to see him."

A few minutes later, she left a rather bewildered-looking Inspector Witherspoon with Mrs. Crookshank. Luty Belle was still talking when Mrs. Jeffries left the terrace.

*   *   *

Mrs. Jeffries waited till lunch was over before she began. The little chat she'd had with Betsy that morning, coming on top of Smythe's less-than-subtle hints, had convinced her that her attempts to discreetly help the inspector with his cases weren't fooling anybody.

"I've called you all together," she said, "because I need to . . . shall we say, clarify a situation of which I'm sure you're all already fully aware. It concerns the inspector and, of course, his cases."

Smythe gave her a cocky grin, Betsy giggled, Mrs. Goodge nodded and Wiggins looked confused.

Feeling suddenly very guilty, Mrs. Jeffries cleared her throat. "As some of you may have guessed, sometimes, the inspector . . ." She faltered, not wanting to come right out and say the dear man was a bit slow when it came to crime.

"Don't know what he's doin'," volunteered Betsy.

"Is a bit thick," interjected Smythe.

"Has his head in the clouds," stated Mrs. Goodge.

"Huh?" said Wiggins.

"Really," Mrs. Jeffries said, suddenly defensive of her inspector. "He's not that bad."

"No disrespect intended," Smythe said smoothly.

"Oh no, he's a wonderful gentleman, is our inspector," Betsy said quickly.

"They don't come any finer," Mrs. Goodge agreed.

"Well, yes, I'm delighted all of you feel that way," Mrs. Jeffries continued. "As I was saying, sometimes the inspector has some very difficult cases, and occasionally, he needs our help. It's very gratifying that you've all grasped that so quickly and without my having to come out and ask for your assistance."

"A bit hard to miss, if you ask me," Smythe put in. "Ever since those Kensington High Street murders you've been sending me round to half the pubs in London to pick up bits and pieces for ya."

"And I do so appreciate all your efforts, as I'm sure the inspector would too," Mrs. Jeffries paused and then said meaningfully, "if he knew about it."

"Is that what this is all about, then?" Betsy asked. "You don't want us lettin' on to the inspector that we's helps out." She shook her head. "You don't have to worry none about that. We knows how to keep our traps shut. All of us think the world of him, so we're not likely to say anything."

"Certainly not," Mrs. Goodge seconded.

"Say something about what?" Wiggins looked even more confused.

"About running all over London gettin' information on the inspector's cases, you dunderhead," Smythe exploded. "What do you think Mrs. J has been up to when she sends you running off to Mudie's Circulating Library or following some toff?"

"Oh," Wiggins's face lit up in a smile. "Is that what's been goin' on, then? I was wondering."

Mrs. Goodge mumbled into her teacup, and Mrs. Jeffries could only make out the words "thick as two short planks."

"So we're all agreed, then?" she asked. "We'll continue helping our inspector and we won't say a word about it?" She gazed quizzically around the table.

They all solemnly nodded their agreement. Smythe cocked his chin to one side and asked, "Why'd you not tell us right off? Did ya think we wouldn't be willing to help the man?"

"No," she sighed, "that wasn't it at all. I suppose I was worried that you'd resent it, or feel that I was asking you to do things that weren't part of the normal household tasks."

"Resent it?" exclaimed Betsy. "We love it. Believe me, dashing about findin' clues is a lot more interestin' than polishing the silver."

"That's for sure," Smythe muttered. He looked down at his big hands for a moment and then back up at Mrs. Jeffries. "All right, what's next then? Are we on to something with this Slocum case?"

Mrs. Jeffries swallowed the sudden lump in her throat. Her instincts about them had been right. They all had their own reasons for being devoted to Inspector Witherspoon:

Betsy, an untrained orphan, whom he'd found huddled and sick in a back alley and brought home for Mrs. Jeffries to nurse.

Smythe and Wiggins, whom he'd saved from probable unemployment by keeping them on after his Aunt Euphemia died. And he'd needed them about as much as he needed that odious Inspector Nivens dodging his every footstep.

Mrs. Goodge, who'd become slow and arthritic and destined for who-knew-what, before Witherspoon offered her a job as his cook.

And herself. A lonely widow from Yorkshire with a passion for mysteries and a need to mother the whole world. Yes, she thought happily, they'd all do quite well.

"Mrs. Jeffries." Betsy's voice brought her out of her reveries. The girl sat up straighter in her starched uniform and smoothed a curl off her shoulder. "About Dr. Slocum?"

"Yes. Let's see." She glanced at the coachman. "Smythe, I'm afraid I'll have to ask you to make the supreme sacrifice and go back to that awful pub in Knightsbridge."

He groaned and then nodded agreement. "To find out what?"

"Anything you can about the Slocum household. How many servants were employed there, who they were and what their jobs were. We need to know what's going to happen to them now. And if you can, find out who inherits the Slocum estate."

She also gave him the names of the others who'd been present at Luty Belle Crookshank's tea party on Saturday and told him to see what he could find out about those people. In doing so, she explained about the poisoned mushrooms growing in the communal gardens and that everyone present at the party knew about them.

"That it?" Smythe rose to his feet.

Mrs. Jeffries tapped her finger against her chin. "See if

you can find out if anything unusual happened that day. *Anything,* no matter how trivial."

She turned to Wiggins. "I want you to go to Knightsbridge this afternoon," she told him. "See if you can make the acquaintance of any of the servants who are employed by any of the guests at that party on Saturday. But for goodness' sake, be discreet. Inspector Witherspoon is still at Dr. Slocum's, and we don't want him seeing you."

"But that'll take me all afternoon," Wiggins protested.

"Did you have other plans?" she asked archly.

"I wanted to finish cleaning out front," he stammered.

"Humph," Betsy snorted. "You don't care a fig about your cleaning; you just don't want to miss seeing that Miss Cannonberry."

"That's not true."

"Get on with you, boy," Mrs. Goodge said. "There's lots of pretty girls to turn your head in Knightsbridge."

Wiggins sighed but got to his feet.

"What do you want me to do?" Betsy asked. Her eyes were shining with eagerness.

"I want you to go with Wiggins," Mrs. Jeffries said briskly. "But once there, you'll need to start talking to all the clerks and tradesmen in the area—just as you did that time on the Kensington High Street."

"But what should I ask?"

"Just get them talking," she replied. "Right now, we're not sure about what we need to know. Find out if Dr. Slocum paid his bills promptly, if he was well liked; find out anything you can. We'll sort out what's important and what's not later."

A few minutes later they left the kitchen, and Mrs. Jeffries found herself alone with the cook.

Mrs. Goodge was a tall, gray-haired woman with painful arthritis and a somewhat cranky disposition at times. She was also a snob. Yet at the same time, she was also kindhearted and generous—some would say overly generous, as Mrs. Jeffries had several times found her feeding beggars at the back door. Naturally, the housekeeper had pretended to notice nothing—she knew Mrs. Goodge valued her testy reputation. The cook also had another, rather startling, quality.

She knew everything there was to know about everyone worth knowing about. Not a tidbit of gossip, not a breath of scandal ever escaped her eager ear. There was nothing particularly startling in that except for one very important fact. Mrs. Goodge never left the kitchen. Except for retiring to her quarters at the back of the house every night, the woman was never outside her domain. Not even to go to church.

"Can I make you a fresh cup of tea?" Mrs. Jeffries asked. "I saw you limping earlier, and I can see your arthritis is acting up again."

The cook nodded regally. "I'd be much obliged."

"We'll put another poultice on your ankle tonight before you go to bed. Perhaps that'll help ease the pain a bit."

"Thank you. The last one you fixed worked wonders. Better than that stuff old McCromber tried to foist off on me."

Old McCromber was the Witherspoon household physician.

Mrs. Goodge considered him a silly old fool, and Mrs. Jeffries wasn't sure but that she agreed with that assessment. The man was too overly fond of laudanum to her way of thinking.

"Mrs. Goodge," she said as she went to the stove to put the kettle on. "Do you know anything about Dr. Slocum?"

"What's his full name?"

"Bartholomew Slocum."

"Let me think a minute," Mrs. Goodge ordered. She stared into space, her face grave in concentration. Several minutes passed, and the teakettle whistled.

Mrs. Jeffries grabbed the kettle and poured the boiling water into the china pot just as Mrs. Goodge spoke.

"I'm sorry," she said. "Could you repeat what you said?

I'm afraid the kettle was making so much noise I didn't hear you."

"It'll keep till the tea's ready."

A few minutes later, Mrs. Jeffries set a steaming cup under the cook's nose and then sat down in chair beside her with her own cup. "Now, what were you saying about Dr. Slocum?"

Mrs. Goodge took a dainty sip of tea. "Nothing."

"Nothing," Mrs. Jeffries repeated, her astonishment obvious. "Does that mean you don't know anything about the man?"

"Afraid so." Mrs. Goodge reached for a digestive biscuit off the plate in the middle of the table. "He's not really anyone important. He's only a doctor and a common one at that."

"Oh dear," Mrs. Jeffries replied. She was very disappointed. She'd been hoping for something to sink her teeth into, a bit of scandal or old gossip. But if Mrs. Goodge didn't know anything about the man, that could very well mean there wasn't anything worth knowing. Drat.

"No, no. I've never heard a word about Dr. Slocum. But I know a lot about Effie Beals."

"Effie Beals?" Mrs. Jeffries perked up. "Who is that?"

Mrs. Goodge smiled, taking pleasure in showing off her knowledge. "Dr. Slocum's cook."

CHAPTER 4

Mrs. Jeffries breathed a sigh of relief. Anything, no matter how small, might help. She gazed expectantly at Mrs. Goodge. "Why how very clever of you," she said. "But then, you're quite remarkable when it comes to learning about what is going on in this city. Tell me what you know about the cook."

"It's not all that much," Mrs. Goodge said modestly. "But it caused a right ripple when it happened."

"When what happened?" Mrs. Jeffries asked patiently, resisting the urge to hurry the woman along. Mrs. Goodge enjoyed the telling of it far too much. She hoarded her tidbits of gossip like an old miser with a pot of gold.

"Why, Effie Beals leaving the Duke of Bedford and going to work for a common doctor." Mrs. Goodge's delicate snort showed what she thought of such strange behavior. "I never heard of the like before in all my days. Leaving a duke to work for a doctor. Monstrous, that's what it was, absolutely monstrous."

Mrs. Jeffries would hardly have labeled it monstrous, but she kept her opinion to herself. "Perhaps," she ventured, "the duke wasn't a very good employer?"

"Not a good employer!" Mrs. Goodge exclaimed, her eyes widening and her whole body swelling indignantly. "Of course he's a good employer. Look 'ere, my sister's husband's cousin is a footman in his Lordship's London house; there isn't a better master alive than the duke." She shook her head. "No, I tell you, something peculiar must have happened. Nobody in their right mind gives up good wages and a fancy roof over their heads unless something inn't right."

"Perhaps she was asked to leave. Perhaps her culinary skills failed to keep up with the duke's standards."

The cook shook her head. "No, that weren't it. I heard the duke himself tried to talk her out of leaving."

"But, Mrs. Goodge, there could be any number of reasons for changing employment."

"Like what?"

"Improprieties, or perhaps she didn't get along with the rest of the servants. Or perhaps it was simply too much responsibility for the poor woman. Cooking for a lord of the realm must be quite daunting."

"Effie Beals is one of the best cooks in London. She worked there for years before she up and left," Mrs. Goodge countered. "Her own daughter was training for the duke's service. No one ever leaves the duke's household—he's a kind, thoughtful and generous man. I tell you, somethin' peculiar happened to that woman, either that or she isn't right in the head. You don't just up and walks away from a position like that to go work for some nobody doctor in Knightsbridge."

Mrs. Jeffries nodded thoughtfully. She wasn't sure Mrs. Goodge was right, but all the same, it was peculiar. Why had Effie Beals left the Duke of Bedford to go to work for Dr. Slocum? It was an interesting question, but one which probably had no relevance to Slocum's murder.

"People leaves their jobs for two reasons," Mrs. Goodge said. "Rotten wages or rotten treatment. Take my word for it," she said firmly. "Neither of them reasons is the right one for Effie Beals."

Witherspoon's ears were ringing by the time he escaped from the garrulous Luty Belle Crookshank. Taking Constable Barnes, he hurried off to question the neighbors before Mrs. Crookshank could remember anything else to tell him.

Witherspoon didn't relish talking to Colonel Seaward. Rumor had it that the man was being tapped as the next governor to one of those horridly hot little islands out in the West Indies. In the inspector's experience, people like that didn't much care for being questioned in murder investigations.

But it couldn't be helped. Witherspoon sighed heavily as they climbed the stone steps to the front door. Regardless of how unpleasant this might be, he had his duty to do.

The butler opened the door and they stated their business. The servant didn't blink an eye. He sent Barnes with a housemaid off to the servants' hall and then told the inspector that Colonel Seaward was in his study.

A few moments later, Witherspoon stopped just inside the study door and blinked in surprise. The most peculiar objects he'd ever seen filled every available inch of the large room.

There were tables scattered about, covered with exotic fringed cloth and topped by woven baskets, multicolored pottery jars and other knickknacks he didn't even recognize.

On the far wall, the head of a tiger stared at him impassively. Next to that was what looked like some sort of African shield with crossed spears at the top. Slowly, Witherspoon turned his head, surveying the room like a child studying the window of a toy shop.

There were more shields and spears on the walls, as well as four fearsome-looking African masks and a wickedly sharp set of ivory knives. He counted three cases of mounted butterflies and six brightly stuffed birds. Next to the window, he saw a bookcase topped with a row of glass cases.

Squinting, he gulped when he saw what they contained: spiders, snakes, lizards and bugs. Witherspoon suppressed a shudder. He hated creepy crawly things. Without taking his gaze off the window, he moved in the opposite direction and banged his foot against something.

"Egad," Witherspoon shouted as he looked down and then leapt to one side. He'd run into a giant crocodile.

"Don't worry, it's dead," said a voice.

Witherspoon tore his eyes away from the hideous creature and saw a man rising from behind a desk in a shadowy corner of the room. "Colonel Seaward," he croaked. "I'm Inspector Witherspoon of Scotland Yard."

"Sorry about that," the colonel replied, gesturing at the stuffed animal. "I hope it didn't startle you too badly."

Seaward was a tall, impeccably dressed man wearing a black morning coat and vest. He had thinning auburn hair streaked with gray, a pencil-thin mustache and an anxious smile.

"I do keep some live reptiles out at my country house," he continued, his gaze on the inspector's pale face. "But I assure you, sir, that one is definitely dead."

"Of course," Witherspoon replied. "Bit of a shock, but not to worry, I'm fine now."

"I expect you've come to see me about that dreadful business at Dr. Slocum's. Won't you please sit down." Seaward nodded toward a chair and went back behind the desk.

"Yes, I have," the inspector replied breathlessly. "If you don't mind, I'd like to ask you a few questions. All routine, I assure you."

"Certainly. Though I don't think there's much I'll be able to tell you. I wasn't all that well acquainted with Dr. Slocum."

Trying to slow down his racing heart, the inspector took a deep breath and cleared his throat. "Were you a patient of the deceased?"

"Not really," the colonel replied. "I did see him professionally once, but that was years ago, when I left the military."

"I see. So he was just a neighbor, not really a close friend?"

"Yes, but . . ." Seaward smiled slightly, as though he wanted to add something but was too much of a gentleman.

"But?" Witherspoon queried.

"One doesn't like to speak ill of the dead. But I must say, Dr. Slocum wasn't really the sort of person one would wish to spend one's time with, if you know what I mean."

"Hmmm, yes. Yet you were at Mrs. Crookshank's tea party last Saturday and Dr. Slocum was there."

"Of course," Seaward gave him a wide man-to-man smile. "It's impossible to refuse one of Mrs. Crookshank's invitations; she's a rather determined woman. But for the most part, I, and everyone else around here, avoided the man like the plague."

"Mrs. Crookshank happened to mention that you're out in the garden a great deal of the time. Did you happen to notice any strangers lurking about on Wednesday? Or anything else that struck you as unusual?"

"Wednesday? Oh yes, the day Slocum died." Seaward's thin eyebrows drew together. "No, I'm afraid I didn't. But that's to be expected. You see, as soon as I could decently leave Mrs. Crookshank's tea, I left for my country estate in Surrey. I didn't get back until Wednesday. I had guests coming to luncheon, and I only just got here ahead of them." He laughed. "My butler was most annoyed. Poor fellow probably thought he was going to have to entertain Lord and Lady Stanhope on his own."

The inspector smiled faintly. "When did your guests leave?"

"Let me see, we finished luncheon a little after one-thirty, chatted for a bit and then they left at. . . ." He cocked his head to one side. "It must have been just after two. I remember because Mrs. Melton kept looking at the clock. She had an appointment at two-thirty. Would you like the names of my guests?"

"That would be most helpful," the inspector replied. Goodness, he thought, this was turning out to be a most interesting interview. He must remember to tell Mrs. Jeffries about this room. She'd find it fascinating. And wasn't he lucky that Colonel Seaward was being so cooperative. Not at all like some he'd had to question.

The colonel pulled a sheet of paper out of a drawer and began scribbling names.

"I assure you," Witherspoon said earnestly, "this is all routine. But we will need to contact your guests to see if any of them heard or saw anything on the day of the murder."

Seaward stood up and handed him the list of names. "Of course, I understand; you're doing your duty. We must all do our duty, mustn't we?"

"Yes indeed." The inspector tucked the paper into his pocket and rose to his feet. "I understand congratulations might soon be in order."

"Perhaps," Seaward murmured with a modest smile. "We shall see what happens when Her Majesty returns from Balmoral next week. I have it on good authority that the Palace will be announcing several appointments at that time." He broke off and frowned slightly. "Do you think you'll have this matter sorted out by then?"

"Hmm, I'm not sure. But one certainly hopes so."

Mrs. Jeffries pounced on Witherspoon the moment he came in. "My goodness, Inspector," she said, holding the front door open and ushering him inside, "you're soaked."

"Good evening, Mrs. Jeffries," Witherspoon said brightly. He shook the rain off himself and unbuttoned his coat. "Foul evening out there."

Mrs. Jeffries rushed forward and grabbed the garment as he shrugged out of it. Surreptitiously, she felt his pockets as she hung it on the brass coatrack.

She didn't usually violate a person's privacy by fingering his pockets, but in the inspector's case, she'd long since come to terms with her conscience over the matter.

Witherspoon needed all the help he could get. Frequently, what was or was not in his coat gave her the means to assist him without having to hurt the dear man's feelings by being blatant about it.

"Started to rain the instant I left the Brompton Road," Witherspoon continued, "and it hasn't let up since. Naturally, there wasn't a hansom to be found. Amazing how they're never around when you need them."

"Poor man, you must be chilled to the bone," Mrs. Jeffries clucked.

"Not to worry, a little bit of water won't hurt me. What delight is Mrs. Goodge cooking up for dinner tonight?" He rubbed his hands together. "I must say I've quite an appetite."

"It's one of your favorites, Inspector. Roast chicken. But come into the drawing room and have a nice glass of sherry first. We don't want you catching a chill—not in the middle of a case."

Witherspoon followed her into the drawing room, his eyes lighting up with pleasure when he saw the two glasses poured out and sitting atop the mahogany table by his favorite armchair. A fire was burning in the fireplace. "Splendid. You're going to join me then."

"I thought perhaps that would be nice." She handed him a glass and picked up her own. "Dinner will be ready in a few minutes, but why don't you tell me about your day? How is the case going?"

The inspector began telling her about his interview with Colonel Seaward. He described the fantastic room, told her about the glass cases and the mounted butterflies and the African masks. She listened carefully, every now and then asking him a question.

"So he provided you with a list of the guests who were there on Wednesday," she remarked thoughtfully. "I suppose you'll have to question them. Even though it's quite usual in a case like this, I expect it might be a bit embarrassing for the colonel."

"Not if I can help it," Witherspoon vowed. "If the servants verify that the colonel was with his guests until two o'clock, then I won't have to embarrass the man by questioning his guests. I should know tomorrow. Barnes was still over there taking their statements when I left."

"You think Colonel Seaward's innocent because he can account for his time during the period the murder was committed?"

"Not just that." Witherspoon took a sip of sherry. "The man had no reason to kill Dr. Slocum. He barely knew him, and from everything he said, he avoided him as much as possible. Besides, the man is a *gentleman.* Furthermore, we have found someone who did have a motive to murder the doctor. Someone in his own household."

"Who?"

"Dr. Slocum's cook. Effie Beals."

"Really?" She hid her surprise behind a smile. "What leads you to that conclusion?"

"Simple. One of the housemaids told me she overheard the cook having a violent argument with the deceased not ten minutes before lunch. Mrs. Beals could easily have known about the mushrooms because Mrs. Crookshank had told the gardener, in front of several witnesses and goodness knows how many servants, that there were poisoned mushrooms in the garden. In a fit of rage, Effie Beals dashed out to the garden, plucked one and popped it into Slocum's soup."

"How abominable!" Mrs. Jeffries paused for a moment and then said, "But what about the second mushroom, the one you found in the cooling pantry?"

He dropped his gaze and stared into his glass. "Hmm, yes. Well, that was probably a spare, in case the first one didn't work."

"You think so? But even if Mrs. Beals did have an argument with her employer, it doesn't necessarily follow that she'd murder him."

"Well, she didn't much like him," Witherspoon mused.

"Did the rest of the servants?"

"Not particularly. So far, I haven't found anyone who liked the man."

"If he was so heartily disliked by everyone who knew him," Mrs. Jeffries ventured, "perhaps there's more to this case than you've discovered so far."

"I don't think so," Witherspoon insisted. "It looks very clear to me. Mrs. Beals is the only one who could have done it. Perhaps she had some sort of fit or something. All the other servants were gone and the house was empty. The doors were locked. There weren't any strangers lurking in the neighborhood, and by the time the poisoned mushroom was added to the doctor's soup, the only person in the house was Effie Beals." He shook his head. "No, let's not make this more complicated than it already is. I think we've found our killer. I've left a constable on duty at the Slocum house to make sure our suspect doesn't do a flit in the middle of the night. I'll be questioning her tomorrow."

"No doubt, you're absolutely right." Mrs. Jeffries knew the inspector believed he'd solved the case. But she also knew that no matter how much he wanted to believe it was over and done with, if she kept asking the right questions and nudging him in the right direction, he'd keep right on investigating. She deliberately frowned.

Witherspoon's satisfied air disappeared. "Why are you looking like that?"

"Like what?" she asked innocently.

"Like you've just thought of something."

"I must admit, I'm puzzled. You said the doctor had an emetic clutched in his hand when you got there," she explained, hoping he'd pick up on her reasoning.

"Yes," he said encouragingly, "he did. But what's that got to do with it?"

"Doesn't that imply he knew he'd been poisoned? And if he knew he'd been poisoned, he must have had some inkling as to why." She held her breath.

"I suppose one could make that assumption," he admitted cautiously.

"Well, if his argument with Mrs. Beals was so violent that he felt she was dangerous, why didn't he sack her right then and make her leave the house? Did the housemaid say Mrs. Beals had been let go?"

"Er, no." Witherspoon's shoulders slumped. "But the maid might not have known. He could have sacked the cook and that's why she killed him! Yes, I'm sure that's probably it. He fired her and she decided to kill him."

"Then why did she return to the house that night? If one has been fired and then murdered one's employer, I'd expect the last thing one would do is return to the scene of the crime and wait to be arrested."

"Er, well, look, Mrs. Jeffries. You may have a point there." He sighed and put his glass on the table. "Drat. I was so hoping this would be a nice simple one. But I daresay, unless the cook is a half-wit, you're probably right. Mrs. Beals wouldn't have come back to the house if she'd killed him. I suppose I'll just have to keep on looking. But honestly, she's the only suspect I've got."

"Don't look so glum, Inspector," Mrs. Jeffries said firmly. "You haven't failed yet in the cause of justice. I know you'd rather shoot yourself in the foot than send an innocent person to the gallows. Besides, you've still got all the other neighbors to question. Perhaps one of them saw something useful."

The mantel clock struck six. Witherspoon reached into his pocket, pulled out his watch and checked the time, then absently set it down on the table.

Mrs. Jeffries and the inspector rose at the same time.

"Dinner should be ready now," she said, eyeing the watch. Witherspoon straightened and hurried toward the hall and the dining room. She waited until he was halfway across the room and then quickly snatched the watch and dropped it in the pocket of her dress.

Tomorrow she had to talk to Effie Beals.

"Inspector," she called as she followed him into the dining room. "Did you speak with the maid again?"

Witherspoon paused, his hand on the back of his chair. "Maid?"

"Yes, remember, you mentioned that it might be pertinent to find out when the surgery had been cleaned?"

"Oh yes, I did say that, didn't I? As a matter of fact, I talked to her this afternoon." He frowned, remembering the plain, uncooperative woman who'd stared at him with her unblinking black eyes and her mouth curled up in a permanent sneer. Most uncomfortable. For the life of him, he couldn't understand why some people seemed to hate the police.

"And?"

He pulled the chair out and sat down, his attention focused on the steaming plates of food. "And what?"

"What did she say?" Mrs. Jeffries managed to keep the impatience out of her voice. "When was the room last cleaned?"

"The morning of the murder." Witherspoon helped himself to some roast chicken and managed to splatter gravy on the white lace tablecloth. Mrs. Jeffries glided to the table and deftly picked up his plate. Within seconds she had heaped it full of food, and all without more damage to the tablecloth. She set it under the inspector's nose and then sat down next to him. Honestly, she thought, when he was hungry, it was difficult to get him to concentrate on anything.

She waited until he'd taken several mouthfuls and then said, "So it was cleaned that morning. Was that the usual routine in the household?"

"Oh yes, the woman told me Slocum was a stickler for cleanliness. She said he watched her like a hawk, and if he even found one speck of dust anywhere, he, in her words, 'had a royal fit,' whatever that is." He reached for the potatoes and plonked another one on his plate before Mrs. Jeffries could intervene. The drippings landed halfway between his plate and the bowl. She gave up any hope of saving the tablecloth.

"I showed her the piece of cork," he continued, "and she's sure it wasn't there that morning. She swept the entire room, including underneath all the cabinets and cupboards, and she's certain it wasn't there. Claims the doctor would have noticed."

"Perhaps someone dropped it on the floor after the maid had cleaned," Mrs. Jeffries suggested.

"Not likely. Except for cleaning the surgery, none of the servants were ever allowed to go in there. Slocum was adamant about that. Fired a housemaid once for wandering in and having a peek at his books."

"Perhaps Dr. Slocum himself dropped it or tracked it in on his shoe?"

Witherspoon shook his head. "No. He wasn't seeing patients that day. According to the maid and the butler, he wasn't in his surgery at all. Except for going out briefly that morning, Slocum was in his study." He snorted delicately. "If you ask me, the old boy was a bit of a martinet. But then, one can't really blame him—at least not when it comes to keeping his surgery clean. But I don't like the way he treated his servants. I tell you, Mrs. Jeffries, none of them are in the least bit upset over the man's death. Except, of course, they're all wondering what will happen to them now that he's gone."

"What will happen to them?" she asked idly, her mind still on that small piece of cork. If it hadn't been there that morning, then there were only two people who could have dropped it. Slocum or the murderer.

"Right now, nothing. His solicitor is keeping the servants on until the estate's settled. That won't be for another fortnight."

"Goodness, what's taking so long?"

"The solicitor's been ill—fellow's had the gout for a month now. Dashed nuisance for the heirs, I'd imagine."

"Heirs?" That perked her ears up. "Who inherits?"

For a moment, she was positively furious at her own stupidity. The question of who was going to get all the doctor's worldly goods was the first thing she should have found out! She couldn't believe she'd been so obtuse. "I understood the man didn't have a family."

"He didn't have much of one, just a nephew hanging about somewhere. I'll know more after I've seen the solicitor, I'm seeing him tomorrow. Gout or not, I've got to get the details about Dr. Slocum's will." He frowned and absently stared across the room. "You know how these solicitors are. He may balk at giving me any useful information. Well, I shall just have to impress upon him that in a murder investigation, it's rather important that we know who's going to get the estate. Motive, you know. Yes, that's what I'll do. I'll simply insist, if necessary." He gazed at Mrs. Jeffries anxiously. "Gout's not catching, is it?"

"No, Inspector. It isn't."

Relieved, he reached for his wine, took a sip and leaned back in his chair. "I say, this is a jolly good dinner. Mrs. Goodge has really outdone herself, hasn't she?"

Mrs. Jeffries sat up late that night, reading the book on mushrooms that Wiggins had gotten from Mudie's Circulating Library. But it wasn't much help. There was practically nothing in it about "Death Caps" or, as Mrs. Crookshank called them, "dead eyes."

Holding the open book in her lap, Mrs. Jeffries closed her eyes and let her mind wander over what few facts she had about the case. Somehow, she didn't think Mrs. Effie Beals was the culprit. If the cook had done it, she would have to be a half-wit to come back to the house that evening and wait to be arrested, especially with that second mushroom sitting in the midst of the cook's domain—the cooling pantry. No one was that stupid.

Her mind drifted back and forth over everything the inspector had told her. But there was still so much she and the other servants needed to find out. Except for her fortuitous meeting with Mrs. Crookshank, none of them had learned all that much today.

Betsy had popped in after dinner to report that she hadn't had any luck getting anyone to talk about Slocum, but she was determined to go back the next day and have another go at it.

Smythe showed up, and he too had nothing to report. Wiggins probably hadn't fared any better than the other two, Mrs. Jeffries thought, but she'd have to wait until tomorrow to find out. The boy had declared himself dead tired and trotted off to bed directly after dinner.

Opening her eyes, Mrs. Jeffries straightened her spine and took a deep breath. She needed to get to sleep. Tomorrow was going to be a busy day.

It was mid-morning before Mrs. Jeffries was able to track Wiggins down. Sometimes she rather thought she'd become a bit too lax in the household management. No doubt some would say her methods were the sad result of too liberal an education for a female, but she didn't bother herself overly much with others' opinions. Yet she did often wonder what she would have been like had she not been exposed to the philosophical writings of John Locke and the poetry of the American Mr. Walt Whitman. (Many, were, of course, scandalized by Mr. Whitman's poems, but she found them thought-provoking and rather charming.)

And as to her household management, well, she always hated having anyone looking over her shoulder as she worked.

So when she first came to the inspector, she had devised a revolutionary, at least in her opinion, system to keep the household running smoothly. She'd sat down with everyone and made a list of all their duties and responsibilities. She'd then told them it was up to them to see that everything got done.

Along with that, she'd also encouraged free expression, personal liberty and a respect for everyone's privacy. Unlike in most households, she didn't think it her business to inquire as to what the servants did on their days off, what their religious preferences were or how they spent their wages.

But as she spied Wiggins heading down the hall with a bucket of water, intent upon cleaning the fence again, she wondered if she'd gone too far. Perhaps some people simply weren't ready for unsupervised responsibility. That fence didn't need another cleaning.

"Wiggins," she called from the top of the staircase. "Where are you going with that bucket? The fence has already been done."

He flushed guiltily. "Uh, uh, I was going to clean the front steps."

"They don't need to be cleaned either," she said calmly, coming down the staircase and pinning him with her steely gaze. "You did them the day before yesterday."

"I did?" he said innocently. "I must have forgotten."

"Wiggins," she sighed, "I know you like to perch out front in the hopes of seeing one of your lady love's walk past. But there isn't anything out there that needs doing. So far this week, you've cleaned the stairs, washed the fence and swept the walkway. Twice. You've also polished the brass door knocker and the lamps to such a brightness it's a miracle we haven't blinded people. But, dear boy, you have many other duties. The rugs need to be beaten."

"But, Mrs. Jeffries," he protested, "them rugs have to be done out back, and I ain't seen her for the longest time."

Mrs. Jeffries wondered which "her" he was referring to, but wasn't sure she wanted to ask.

"Yesterday you had me running all over ha'f o' London getting the goods on them tea party guests."

"Speaking of which," she interjected cheerfully, "what did you find out?"

He snorted. "Not much. If you ask me, it was a right waste of time. But I did find out that Mrs. Leslie has a French maid, right stuck-up one too, and that Dr. Hightower hangs around that neighborhood like he lives there, an' he don't."

"Anything else?"

"I 'eard all about that Colonel Seaward," Wiggins replied wearily. "Right boring ol' toff too, if you ask me."

"Well done, Wiggins," Mrs. Jeffries said. "How clever of you. How did you manage that and, more importantly, what precisely did you find out?"

The boy grinned as she praised him. He straightened and puffed his chest out importantly. "I hung around the side of Seaward's house until I saw one of the maids come out, then I follows her to the butcher."

"Excellent," Mrs. Jeffries murmured.

"Anyways, this maid, her name was Sophie, she wan't much to look at, but she was a nice enough girl and a real chatterbox. I asked if I could carry her basket back to the house. Clever, huh?"

"Very," she replied dryly. She did wish he would get to the point, but she also realized that, like Mrs. Goodge, he needed to feel his contribution to the inspector's case was important.

"Sophie says the colonel's an old army officer, but he's not in the army now. I asked Sophie if the colonel was acquainted with the doctor, if they was friends like, and she said no. Said Colonel Seaward didn't like the man much."

"From what I've heard, no one liked the doctor very much."

"That's the truth," he agreed, nodding his head. "Sophie says no one round there had much to do with 'im, even if he was always droppin' them fancy little callin' cards at people's houses."

"Calling cards?" Mrs. Jeffries's brows drew together. "Are you saying that Dr. Slocum dropped off his calling card at Colonel Seaward's and at other homes in the neighborhood?"

"That's what Sophie says. But no one round there liked 'im much. She said Dr. Slocum could clear the neighbors out the garden faster than a bad smell. But that didn't stop him from going round and tryin'. It's funny, inn't? Even on the day he was murdered he'd dropped one o' them fancy little cards by Colonel Seaward's. Sophie says she thought ol' Slocum wanted to be invited to lunch."

"What?" Mrs. Jeffries said sharply. "You mean he sent his calling card around on the day he was killed?"

"That's what Sophie says, and she ought to know. She's the one he give it to when he came round that morning."

CHAPTER 5

Witherspoon stood impatiently next to the settee in Catherine Leslie's drawing room and waited. He'd been waiting a good ten minutes now, he thought irritably as he glanced at the clock on the marble mantelpiece. What on earth was taking that blasted maid so long? He didn't have all day. There was so much to do this morning. Effie Beals had to be questioned again and then he had to go see Dr. Slocum's solicitor, and if there was time, he wanted another word with Dr. Hightower.

Oh dear, he was never going to get it all done. He began to pace back and forth. Thank goodness he'd had the foresight to have a quick word with that boy that did the gardening. At least he had some information now, even if he wasn't quite sure what it meant.

"Inspector Witherspoon?"

The sound of the soft, feminine voice startled him. He whirled around and stumbled over his own feet. Witherspoon's eyes widened as he saw Catherine Leslie standing in the doorway.

Tall and slender, she was past the bloom of first youth, yet she was one of the loveliest women he'd ever seen. Her upswept hair was jet black and pulled straight back to frame a perfectly smooth oval face. She had high cheekbones, an aristocratic nose and a full, generous mouth. But it was her eyes that drew one's attention. Deeply set and the color of violets, they watched him warily from across the room.

"Inspector Witherspoon," she repeated softly.

Realizing he was staring, he blushed. "Yes, I'm Inspector Witherspoon. You must be Mrs. Leslie."

She inclined her head and moved gracefully to the settee. "My maid said you wished to ask me some questions. Please sit down."

"Thank you. I'm sorry to have to intrude upon you like this, but as you've no doubt heard, your neighbor, Dr. Slocum, was murdered a few days ago."

"Yes. I know. He was poisoned, wasn't he?"

"Unfortunately, yes."

"I don't really see what it has to do with me," she said. "I'm sorry he's dead, but I hardly knew the man."

"Rest assured, madam," the inspector explained, "we haven't singled you out. We're talking with everyone who lives round these gardens. It's very much the normal course of events in an investigation of this kind."

She glanced at the clock and then gave him a nervous smile. Witherspoon had the feeling she was waiting for something.

"Now," he began briskly, "could you tell me how long you've been acquainted with the deceased?"

"I met Dr. Slocum shortly after I moved here from Birmingham. That was three years ago, after my husband died." She bit her lip and looked toward the mantel again.

"So you've known the deceased for three years." Witherspoon repeated. "Yet you weren't particularly friendly with him, is that correct?"

"That's correct."

"Were you in the garden this last Saturday—at Mrs. Crookshank's tea party?"

"Yes."

"And wasn't Dr. Slocum there as well?"

"Yes, he was, but so were a lot of other people." Mrs. Leslie sighed softly. "Inspector Witherspoon," she began in a tone of clarification, "you must understand. No one around here liked that odious little man. Everyone avoided him as much as possible, but Mrs. Crookshank is an American and somewhat of an eccentric as well. She has rather peculiar notions about hospitality, and she invited everyone who lives on the gardens to her party."

"Yes, I see." Witherspoon paused. "Mrs. Leslie, did you happen to see any strangers in the gardens on Wednesday, just before noon?"

"I don't think so," she answered vaguely. "I spent most of the morning lying down. I wasn't feeling well."

"I'm so sorry to hear that. So you saw or heard nothing out of the ordinary that morning?"

They paused as the maid came in carrying a silver tea tray. "Your tea, madam," she said in a pronounced French accent.

"Thank you, Nanette. Would you care for tea, Inspector?"

"Why, that's very good of you," he replied enthusiastically. "I wouldn't mind a cup."

The maid, a pretty blond-haired girl, gazed speculatively at the inspector for a moment and then picked up the silver pot.

Witherspoon took no notice of the maid, he was watching Catherine Leslie. "So you're saying you didn't know the doctor well at all and had no wish to, is that it?"

She accepted a cup of tea and nodded.

"And Dr. Slocum knew you had no wish to further your acquaintance with him?"

"Yes, I'd made that clear on several occasions."

"Then why, Mrs. Leslie, did Dr. Slocum persist?"

Her brows rose. "I'm afraid I don't know what you mean?"

"I think perhaps you do, madam," Witherspoon insisted. Really, did these people think all policemen were fools? "The gardener told me that on the day Dr. Slocum was murdered he accidentally dropped two calling cards on the path. The boy picked them up, caught up with Slocum and gave them back to him. He then watched him come to this house."

There was a loud crash as the maid dropped the cup of tea she'd just poured for Witherspoon. The steaming liquid spilled directly onto Catherine Leslie's skirt.

"Oh, madam," the maid cried, dropping to her knees and brushing at the material with a linen napkin she'd grabbed off the tray. "I am so clumsy, forgive me. I am so sorry. *Mon dieu,* thees will leave a terrible stain."

"It's all right, Nanette," she answered, motioning her away. "It's only a dress." She looked at Witherspoon and took a deep breath. "Inspector, I don't know what you're talking about. Dr. Slocum did not call here on Wednesday morning."

Nanette gasped, and they both turned to look at her.

"But, madam," the girl said, staring at her mistress out of wide, frightened eyes. "Surely you remember, zee awful man, he came here that morning and he left those two cards. One for you, and one for Dr. Hightower."

"That's enough, Nanette," Mrs. Leslie cried.

"No, madam, I can't let you do eet. I can't let you harm yourself to help *Monsieur le Docteur* Hightower. You must not lie to thees policeman, you must tell zee truth. If you do not, he will think you murdered Dr. Slocum and you are innocent."

"Now, now," Witherspoon interjected, but both women ignored him.

"Nanette, please be quiet. You don't know what you're saying."

"I do know what I am saying," the girl cried. "You must tell thees man zee truth. You must tell him everything."

"Nanette, silence."

"*Mais non,* I will not be silent. I will tell everything, I will tell everything, I will tell about zee nasty *docteur* waving his ugly lettle key in your face, threatening you with lies and—"

"Noooo," Mrs. Leslie screamed, and then she stumbled backward.

Inspector Witherspoon reached out to steady her and then made a grab for her as she collapsed, catching her before she hit the floor. "Oh, dear," he said.

Catherine Leslie had fainted.

Mrs. Jeffries once again made her way to Dr. Slocum's. As she climbed the stairs, she noticed that there was no longer a constable on duty. That was a bit of luck. She didn't think she could pull the wool over Barnes's eyes again. He wasn't a fool.

Clutching Inspector Witherspoon's pocket watch in her hand, she knocked on the door.

A few minutes later, the door opened and a white-haired butler with watery blue eyes peered out. "Good morning, madam."

"Good morning. I'm terribly sorry to disturb you," she said, easing closer to the door. "But I must speak with Inspector Witherspoon."

"Who?"

"Inspector Witherspoon, of Scotland Yard," she repeated patiently, not at all surprised by the butler's reaction. Witherspoon sometimes had that effect on people. Unless he was right under their noses, they tended to forget he was in the house. "I believe he's here this morning."

"Oh, him." The butler's eyes narrowed suspiciously. "Are you from Scotland Yard too? Never heard of a woman peeler before. What da ya want? Are you a neighbor? Some nosy parker that thinks she knows something? If you've come around here to start stirring things up and tellin' tales—"

"No, no, no," Mrs. Jeffries said quickly. She leaned closer and caught the distinct smell of brandy on the man's breath. Holding up the pocket watch, she said, "I've only come to return the inspector's watch. I'm his housekeeper. He left this morning without it, and if I don't get it to him, he'll miss some very important appointments."

The butler made a noise that sounded like a grunt and moved to one side. "Come on in, then," he muttered grudgingly. "Take one of them chairs by the surgery door. I'll go see if I can find the copper. He only arrived a minute ago himself. I'll ask the maid where he's got to."

"Thank you," Mrs. Jeffries said sweetly. How very curious, she thought. The butler was obviously in his cups, and he seemed to be under the impression she was coming in to tell tales. I wonder what kind of tales he's worried about, she thought as she watched him weave slowly down the long hallway. As soon as he'd turned the corner, she leapt quickly to her feet and hurried off to examine the layout of the first floor of the house.

Ignoring the surgery, she stopped at a set of double doors just opposite. Peeking inside, she saw that they led to a large library or study cluttered with bookcases, sofas, tables and reading lamps. There was green-and-white wallpaper on the walls, but every inch seemed to be covered with objects. There were oil paintings of country scenes and horses, gilt mirrors and corner shelves crammed with china figures. Probably Dresden, she decided. There was an ugly bright-red velvet settee and two matching chairs at one end of the room and, directly behind them, a grand piano covered by a garish gold fringed shawl. The room was so overly stuffed with bric-a-brac, it was positively gaudy.

Closing the doors, Mrs. Jeffries went next to the room just off the bottom of the staircase. Inside was a dining room fitted out with an oval rosewood table large enough to seat twelve, a matching sideboard and a huge crystal chandelier.

She heard a shuffle of footsteps from behind the staircase and deduced that the butler had located Inspector Witherspoon. She hurried back to the chair outside the surgery and sat down just in time.

"Sorry that took so long, madam," the butler announced, "but one of the maids said the gentleman was upstairs in the parlor. If you'll follow me, madam. It's this way."

Nodding, she followed him upstairs. He'd obviously regained some of his composure, though he did sway slightly when they reached the top. Perhaps the maid he'd spoken to had reminded him that this was a murder investigation.

They stopped outside a partially open door. There was a chair there too. Mrs. Jeffries sat down. "Thank you so much," she said, keeping her voice low. "I think perhaps I'll wait out here for just a few moments. I don't wish to interrupt the inspector."

"As you wish, madam."

"What is your name?" she asked kindly.

He looked surprised. "Keating, ma'am."

"And have you worked here long?" She kept her voice soft and sympathetic.

"Six years, ma'am," he sighed wearily, "but it seems more than that, seems like I've been here a ruddy lifetime.

After having Catherine Leslie faint and then coping with her hysterical maid, Witherspoon had been sure his day couldn't get any worse. But he'd been wrong. He was getting absolutely nothing useful out of Effie Beals.

He stifled a heavy sigh. He knew Constable Barnes was watching him expectantly, waiting, no doubt, for him to pounce upon the woman with a series of devastatingly clever questions.

He glanced over at his only suspect. She was sitting primly, wearing a neatly pressed white apron over a gray dress and watching him with frightened brown eyes.

Mrs. Beals was a heavy-set woman, well into middle age, with dark brown hair, a round face and a pale complexion. She didn't look like a murderess. Not that Witherspoon knew precisely how a murderess should look, but she was so precisely what a cook should look like that it made him jolly uncomfortable.

Mrs. Jeffries's comments the night before had pricked his conscience. There really was no reason to believe Effie Beals had wanted her employer dead.

Witherspoon cleared his throat. When all else failed, try surprise. "Mrs. Beals, did you poison Dr. Slocum?"

"I never," the woman protested with a vehement shake of her head. "Why would I want to kill 'im?"

"Because you'd had a violent quarrel with him and he was going to sack you."

"Who says? He never sacked me," she insisted. "And I didn't kill 'im. You got no right to accuse me—"

"No one is accusing you of murdering Dr. Slocum," Witherspoon interrupted. "We're merely asking the question." Drat, this was going to be far more difficult than he'd hoped. "All right, once again, could you describe your movements on the day of the murder?"

She sniffed. "How come you don't have everyone else in here, answering your questions? I weren't the only one that had a set-to with him, you know."

"We've spoken to all the other servants, Mrs. Beals. They all said the same thing. You were the last one in the house the day Dr. Slocum was poisoned."

"I've already told you about that—I stayed on because I was goin' to visit me daughter out at Chelmsford and the train didn't leave till two o'clock." Her bosom swelled with indignation. "Why should I hang about some drafty old train station when I can stay right here in the comfort of me own room?"

"Did you see Dr. Slocum after the others had left?"

She shook her head. "No, I left his lunch on the dining table, just like he asked me to."

"What did he have for luncheon?"

"Mushroom soup, lamb chops and some bread and cheese. He told me not to bother with a puddin' and so I didn't."

Witherspoon nodded wisely. "Was there anything else? Something to drink, perhaps?"

"Well, he had his bottle of wine. He was a real stickler for that, made Keating bring up a fresh bottle every day. But that weren't my business, that was Keating's. He was in charge of supplyin' the wine. It was sitting on the sideboard when I brung up the lunch tray. So I knows he had it."

"And how long were you at your daughter's?" Witherspoon asked.

"All afternoon." Mrs. Beals brushed at a stray lock of hair that had slipped from beneath her cap. "I didn't even know the man was dead until I got back that night and the police was here."

Mrs. Jeffries ignored the crick in her neck as she cocked her head closer to the door and strained to catch every word. Keating had disappeared again, and she'd overheard most of the inspector's questions. She sighed as she heard him mumbling softly to Constable Barnes, and then she heard him ask Mrs. Beals for her daughter's address in Chelmsford.

Her hands balled into fists of frustration as his deep voice began asking the same questions all over again. Mrs. Jeffries had to restrain herself from flying into the room and ordering Witherspoon to ask the cook why she'd argued with Dr. Slocum. She straightened suddenly as the butler's laborious footsteps sounded on the stairs again.

"Would you care to come into the kitchen for a cup of tea?" Keating asked politely.

Casting one quick glance at the door, Mrs. Jeffries rose and gave him her most charming smile. "Why thank you, Keating, that's most thoughtful of you."

She followed him down two sets of stairs, through a hall and into the kitchen. Her eyes widened in surprise as she gazed at the room. A long table dominated the center. On the far wall were the usual two sets of sinks the scullery maids must use to do the washing up. Next to that was the largest wooden plate rack Mrs. Jeffries had ever seen. Across from the table, there was a brand new Livingstone iron range, so new the plating still shone, and even more, there was one of those new fangled "gas kitchener's" she'd seen in a Charing Cross shop window.

Keating moved to the range and pulled open the hot box. "I've taken the liberty of warming some buns, ma'am," he announced as he lifted a plate out and set them on the table.

"Thank you," she said again. "I didn't want to disturb the inspector, and I daresay he'll be a bit longer speaking with your cook."

Keating put the buns on the table next to a teapot and cups and sat down next to Mrs. Jeffries. "He must be a good employer, ma'am, if you've come all this way just to return his watch."

She nodded and smiled as the butler poured them each a cup of tea. Satisfaction poured through her. Her little scheme was working. Mrs. Jeffries often marveled at the different talents the good Lord had chosen to bestow on people. Some were blessed with great beauty or tremendous artistic or musical talent, and some, like herself, were blessed with subtler gifts. Why, it was her own special gift that had first got her involved with solving crimes, back when her dear late husband had his first employment with the constabulary in Yorkshire.

People talked to her. They told her things they'd often never revealed to another soul. A bit of interest, a kind smile and before you knew it, they were talking their heads off. With her plump, material figure, gray-streaked auburn hair and sympathetic brown eyes, she knew she probably reminded people of a kindly aunt or a spinster sister.

"Humph," the butler sniffed. "You're right lucky, then. If you've got a good master." He cast a quick glance over his shoulder, presumably to make sure no one was sneaking up on him.

"I take it Dr. Slocum wasn't an easy man to work for," she ventured gently.

"Easy! He was a right old tartar."

Mrs. Jeffries didn't know if it was her unique gift or the brandy the man had consumed earlier that was loosening his tongue, but either way, she didn't want him shutting up now.

"Oh dear," she clucked sympathetically. "That does make one's life difficult, doesn't it? And these days, respectable employment is so hard to find."

He nodded vigorously. "That's the truth. None of us would've stayed if we didn't have to."

"Yes, I quite understand."

"And he wasn't much of a doctor, neither, if you asks me," Keating exclaimed. His face was turning red. "He was mean to his patients too. If they couldn't pay his price, he wouldn't treat 'em."

Another disapproving cluck. "That's dreadful."

"He was a dreadful man. About six months ago one of his old patients from when he was over in Hammersmith came in—it was an elderly gentleman, someone who looked like he'd seen better days. He begged the doctor to attend his wife, but he couldn't pay, so Slocum threw him out."

"How monstrous." Mrs. Jeffries did indeed think it was monstrous, but she also knew it was actually quite a common practice. There were many physicians in London who hardened their hearts to the poor and needy.

"It was, ma'am. He was a pathetic old gentleman, I can tell you that. And he'd once been a good patient of the doctor."

"You knew him?"

"Oh no. I've only been here six years. Slocum had his practice in Hammersmith long before that. But I heards this gentleman remind the doctor of all the patients he'd referred to him when he was just starting out." Keating snorted again. "But it didn't do no good. Dr. Slocum tossed him out anyway."

"Hammersmith," Mrs. Jeffries murmured thoughtfully. "That's not a very nice area. Makes quite a change, doesn't it, from Hammersmith to Knightsbridge?"

"Yes. And he didn't get here because his doctoring skills improved any. Half of his patients still ended up dying," Keating stated flatly. "He got this house an' all because he inherited a packet of money from a relative."

"Really? That's interesting."

"And there's more to that story than meets the eye too, 'cause the old uncle who left it all to him didn't even like him."

"How do you know that?" Mrs. Jeffries asked quickly.

Too quickly, because the butler drew back and gazed at her suspiciously.

"Forgive me," she said softly, giving him an understanding smile. "I forget myself, but well, you're such an interesting person to talk with and one can't help being curious, can one?"

Some, but not all, of the suspicion left Keating's eyes. "I suppose so," he said cautiously. But he didn't answer her question.

She decided to change tactics. "I'm so sorry. You must have had a dreadful few days, and here I am bending your ear with my curiosity. And Dr. Slocum not even buried yet." She clucked sympathetically and shook her head. "Even if he wasn't the kindest of employers, I'm sure you're upset."

"Well," he agreed slowly, "I wouldn't exactly call it upset. More like I'm wondering what's going to happen next."

"No doubt you are, and that, of course, is such a worry."

"Course it is," he echoed, "I'm sixty this next spring, and where am I going to get another position? People wants young men they can train, not old men like me, working for them."

"But surely Dr. Slocum made some provision for you? He must not have been completely heartless—after all, he did give you a day off for no apparent reason."

"How do you know about that?"

"The inspector happened to mention it."

"Oh." Keating smiled cynically. "But don't go thinking he was giving us time off out of the goodness of his heart. He had a reason, all right. He was up to something on those days. We just never figured out what it was. The old tartar didn't do anything unless there was something in it for him."

"You mean this wasn't the first time the doctor had given the staff the day off?"

"He'd done it before, several times. But none of us ever knew why."

One of the maids entered the kitchen and then stopped dead. "You're needed upstairs, Mr. Keating," she said, staring at Mrs. Jeffries. "Constable Barnes wants you to show them the attic."

"I'd better go find Inspector Witherspoon," Mrs. Jeffries interjected as she headed for the stairs herself. She wanted to nab the inspector before he disappeared. "Thank you so much for the tea," she called over her shoulder. "We must do it again sometime."

Inspector Witherspoon was pacing the drawing room when Mrs. Jeffries entered. He didn't look surprised to see her.

"Hello, Mrs. Jeffries," he muttered absently, massaging the sides of his head as he paced. "I've had the most dreadful day."

"Good day, sir," she said. "I'm so sorry to hear that. I've brought you your pocket watch. You left it on the table, and I was sure you'd need it."

Witherspoon stopped pacing and stared at the watch with a puzzled frown. "I left it on the table," he muttered, "but I could have sworn I checked there before I left this morning."

Her conscience gave Mrs. Jeffries a nasty nudge. He had left it on the table, but she'd determined she had to be here today and now she was glad she'd come. She'd learned several interesting facts.

"Well, sir," she said cheerfully, "I shouldn't worry about a trifling thing like that. My, my, isn't this an opulent room."

"Uhmm . . . yes." Witherspoon gave up trying to think. It was giving him a pounding headache. "It is very nice."

"Amazing, isn't it? Dr. Slocum has certainly done well for himself. You know, the butler happened to mention that a mere ten years ago he only had a rather small practice in Hammersmith."

"Really?" Witherspoon looked genuinely surprised by that bit of news. Even he understood the economic differences between the elegance of Knightsbridge and the working-class grit of Hammersmith.

"How is the investigation going?" Mrs. Jeffries drifted to the window and peeked through the white lace curtains to the street below.

Witherspoon sighed deeply. "I'm afraid it's not going well at all," he admitted, giving in to the urge to confide in his understanding housekeeper. "The cook, Effie Beals, doesn't look in the least insane, and she's got absolutely no real motive to want to kill Dr. Slocum. But as there was no one else who had touched his food or was even in the house, I don't know where else to look."

"How distressing." She kept her gaze fixed out the window. "But I'm sure you'll come up with the true culprit. You always do."

"And on top of that, Mrs. Leslie fainted when I was trying to get her to tell me about the calling cards, and then the maid had hysterics, and now I've got to go back and interview them all over again."

"Calling cards?"

"Yes, I don't think they've a thing to do with the murder, but they're one of those niggly little details I've got to try and sort out." He went on to describe his talk with the gardener and his subsequent visit to the Leslie household.

Mrs. Jeffries listened carefully. There was a whole heap of questions the inspector should be asking. But she knew she had to be subtle. "Do you think, perhaps, the doctor left calling cards anywhere else?"

"Hmm, I don't know. It's possible, I suppose. Drat, another thing to do. And I've still got to try and see that solicitor today. Not to mention sending Barnes round to the Yard to check the personal effects of the deceased and see if we can find that wretched key."

"What key?" Mrs. Jeffries asked sharply.

"I don't really know," Witherspoon said. "But the maid mentioned a key just before Mrs. Leslie fainted. I don't recall seeing a key on the body. It might be important, so I'm duty-bound to follow it up." He sighed melodramatically. "Oh dear, where will I find the time?"

"Don't upset yourself, Inspector," Mrs. Jeffries said soothingly. "You'll get to the bottom of this case. You always do."

Her mind was on the key. She went over everything she'd learned so far today, and none of it made sense. There were so many questions she needed to answer. Why did Keating think Dr. Slocum was up to something when he gave the servants the day off? And why had he accused her of telling tales when she'd arrived this morning? What kind of tales? About whom? Why had Catherine Leslie fainted? Where was the key and what did it unlock?

She drew in a sharp breath as her gaze caught a familiar figure walking briskly down the pavement on the other side of the street.

It was Inspector Nivens. If he found her here, he'd start nosing around again, trying to prove that Witherspoon wasn't worth a fig as a detective. He'd like nothing better than to catch her snooping into one of Witherspoon's cases. Nivens wasn't brilliant by any means. But he wasn't stupid either. He reminded her of a fox sniffing around the henhouse. If she weren't careful, he'd find a way in.

Yet there was one more important point she needed to make. Mrs. Jeffries moved away from the window and toward the door. "Well, I hope the solicitor will be helpful. Perhaps you'll find that he's left his entire estate to his servants."

Witherspoon laughed. "I don't think so, Mrs. Jeffries. From what I've found out, he didn't like his servants much and they certainly didn't like him."

"Yes, I daresay you're right. Of course, that makes his behavior on the day of his death even more puzzling."

"Pardon?" he said. He'd lost track of the conversation.

"Why, his giving the servants the day off," she reached the door, pulled it open and turned to face the inspector. If she hurried, she could get down the back stairs and out the kitchen door before Nivens realized she'd been in the house. She only hoped that Witherspoon had enough sense to be discreet about the matter.

"I'm sorry. I don't follow you." Witherspoon looked more puzzled than ever. "What's so strange about his giving his people the day out? I've done it myself on more than one occasion."

"But you're a wonderful employer, Inspector. Dr. Slocum wasn't, and it's peculiar for precisely that reason. It sounds to me as if the man gave his servants time off not to be kind, but to insure that he was here all alone."

She heard voices in the front hall and knew she was running out of time. "Perhaps he wanted to be alone because he didn't want any witnesses to know how he spent his afternoon."

CHAPTER 6

Mrs. Jeffries managed to evade the odious Inspector Nivens by ducking into a doorway and then beating a hasty retreat down the stairs after he'd gone past. She paused by the front door, trying to decide whether to go home and pry more information out of Mrs. Goodge, or duck into the back garden and have a look around. She needed to talk with Effie Beals as well, but this wasn't the best time. Not with Inspector Nivens hanging about.

Decision made, Mrs. Jeffries pulled open the heavy front door and hurried down the stairs.

There was still no sign of Smythe when she arrived back in Upper Edmonton Gardens, but she refused to let it worry her anymore. Smythe was a law unto himself—he'd turn up eventually, and when he did, he'd no doubt have something useful to tell her.

She quickly took off her hat and started for the back stairs. But she hadn't taken two steps when the drawing-room door opened and Betsy's excited voice stopped her.

"Oh, good, you're back. I've been waitin' for you," Betsy announced as she rushed forward, a dust cloth hanging limply in her right hand. Her eyes were sparkling, and her cheeks were flushed with excitement. "Mrs. Jeffries, I've learned ever so much."

"Can it wait for a few moments?" Mrs. Jeffries asked,

edging closer to the back stairs. "I really must have a word with Mrs. Goodge."

"But, Mrs. Jeffries," Betsy protested, "you won't believe what all I've found out. I did just like you told me—I chatted up every shopkeeper and clerk I could find. There wasn't much to learn about Dr. Slocum, but I got me an earful about everyone else livin' round that garden, I can tell you. Just goes to show, you shouldn't give up. Yesterday was a bit of a waste o' time, but today I got right lucky. I asked about everyone who was at that tea party on Saturday." She smiled shyly, her face lighting up with pride.

"Let's sit in the drawing room then," Mrs. Jeffries said. Mrs. Goodge would have to wait.

She turned and led the way toward two velvet-covered chairs next to the window. "All right, Betsy," she said as she settled herself, "what did you find out?"

"Well, like I said, Mrs. Jeffries, none of the tradespeople knew much about Dr. Slocum, except that he haggles over their bills . . ."

"Haggles? You mean he doesn't pay what he owes?"

Betsy nodded. "The butcher says he was always nippin' off a few pence here or a half a shilling there. And the fishmonger told me he'd stopped supplying him last year when Dr. Slocum claimed some kippers he'd sent over was rotten and refused to pay for 'em."

"From what we've learned about the man, that doesn't surprise me." The picture of the murder victim Mrs. Jeffries had been forming in her mind became clearer, more defined. Dr. Bartholomew Slocum seemed to go out of his way to make enemies.

"I also found out that he's not the only one round that ways that people gossips about," Betsy continued excitedly. "Colonel Seaward, the one that lives round the corner, he's got a taste for fine wine, buys it by the caseload and all of it from France too, not at all like Dr. Slocum. The wine merchant's assistant was braggin' that you could sell the doctor any old slog as long as it had a fancy label on the bottle. That's one place old Slocum didn't haggle with. They says he paid his bill every month and in full too." She laughed. "Funny, inn't it? What people seems to think is important. Oh yes, I almost forgot. Colonel Seaward, he's some sort of an . . ." Frowning, she paused. "I can't remember the exact word, but he's one of them people that's always fussin' with strange animals and growing exotic plants in his conservatory. He's an amateur . . . oh something or other."

"Naturalist?" Mrs. Jeffries supplied helpfully. She wondered if Colonel Seaward's exotic plants included mushrooms, and then realized it didn't matter. The mushroom that poisoned Dr. Slocum hadn't come from a conservatory or greenhouse, it had come from the communal garden.

"That's it," Betsy agreed. "The colonel's a bit of an odd one too, if you ask me. Donald Roper, he's the grocer's delivery boy, he told me that the colonel actually tried to hire 'im to catch mice and rats. Said he needed them to feed his snakes. Got a whole slew o' them out at his country house. Well, Donald says he weren't havin' none o' that. He's ever such a nice boy, is Donald. Quite handsome too, not that he's really a boy, he's only a year or two younger than me and—"

"Betsy," Mrs. Jeffries interrupted. "Please, let's not digress. You can tell me all about Donald some other time."

"Oh, sorry," she said with a blush. "Now let me see, where was I? Now I remember. That Catherine Leslie, seems she's carrying on with that Dr. Hightower and he's the one that found the body. That's pretty suspicious, if you ask me."

"Are you sure about that?"

Betsy nodded vigorously. "I heard it from the girl in that fancy dress shop on the corner of Brompton Road. Mrs. Leslie's one of their customers, and Tillie, that's who told me, she sometimes goes to the Leslie house to help with dress fittin's. Tillie reckons that Mrs. Leslie is seeing the

doctor on the sly, though why she should have to be doin'
it on the sly is a wonder to me. She bein' a widow and all.
But then, I guess, the doctor would have to be careful, seein'
as he's a married man." She sighed melodramatically. "It's
such a waste, inn't it? The poor man, I feel so sorry for 'im.
It's a romantic tragedy, that's what it is."

"Whom do you feel sorry for?" Mrs. Jeffries asked with
a puzzled frown.

"Dr. Hightower." Betsy's voice dropped to a whisper.
"His wife is a lunatic. He keeps her at home. Tillie says
he's round Mrs. Leslie's house all the time, but theys have
to be discreet about bein' in love with each other. Course
everyone knows what's goin' on."

"Yes, I expect they do," Mrs. Jeffries murmured thoughtfully. She was silent for a long moment, thinking of everything the girl had told her. Finally, she asked, "Anything
else?"

Betsy pursed her lips. "No, I think that's it. Do you want
me to keep at it?"

There were several things that Mrs. Jeffries needed
to know, but she wasn't sure that Betsy was the one
to send.

She had a feeling that the case was becoming more
complicated. More dangerous. And she didn't know why.

"Yes, but not just yet," she answered slowly as she rose
to her feet. "You've done an excellent job, Betsy. I'm very
proud of you. Give me a day or two to decide what we need
to do next."

The girl blushed a becoming pink. "You just lets me
know when you're ready for me to go out again. This
detectin's excitin' work. I do think I'm startin' to get it
right, aren't I?"

"That you are, my dear," Mrs. Jeffries muttered as she
walked to the door. "That you are."

Mrs. Goodge was rolling pastry when Mrs. Jeffries came
into the kitchen. The cook's face was a mask of concen-

tration as her arthritic hands worked the rolling pin slowly back and forth over the dough.

"What are you making?" the housekeeper asked, stepping up to the table. Unlike in most households, she didn't bother going over the menus with the cook; there was no need. They ran things simply here, and Mrs. Goodge was the queen of this kitchen.

"Steak and kidney pudding," she replied without taking her eyes off her dough.

"Lovely. I'm sure it will be delicious." Mrs. Jeffries decided not to waste any time in preliminaries. She needed to get this case moving a bit faster; Inspector Nivens showing up at the Slocum household was a bad sign.

"Mrs. Goodge," she began firmly, "I need some information."

"About who?"

"Several people. Catherine Leslie, Dr. Sebastian Hightower and a Colonel Clayton Seaward. They're all neighbors sharing the same communal gardens as Dr. Slocum. Do you know anything about any of them?"

Mrs. Goodge put the rolling pin down, dusted off her hands and looked up. "Hmmm . . . ," she mumbled. "Seaward, Leslie and Hightower. Wait a minute, wait a minute, something's coming to me."

"Take your time."

"Seaward, Seaward." Suddenly, the cook's eyes lit up. "I remember now. I've heard of *him*. Oh yes, yes indeed. I know all about Colonel Seaward."

"Excellent."

"He's quite a famous man, you know."

"Really?"

"In some circles, that is," Mrs. Goodge said with a sniff. "But he couldn't possibly have anything to do with that murder. Why he's been decorated by the Queen herself. For bravery."

"How interesting." Mrs. Jeffries tried to mask her impatience. Goodness, how the woman liked dragging out the pertinent details in bits and pieces. "Do go on."

"He was in charge of a military outpost in one of them heathen African countries." She wrinkled her brow. "I can't remember which, though. But he was defending the crown when it happened."

Mrs. Jeffries privately thought he was probably defending English commercial and agricultural interests, but she kept that opinion to herself. She'd noticed that her unorthodox views regarding the British Empire were less than popular with most people. "When what happened?"

"Why, him defending the British garrison almost single-handedly. He was half-dead by the time reinforcements got through." Mrs. Goodge shook her head. "There was a native uprising against us, and Colonel Seaward, he was in charge. He managed to hang on, even after most of his men had been slaughtered, till more troops arrived. He was still at his post, fighting off the savages, when the reinforcements broke through."

"I would hardly refer to the native peoples of another country as savages," Mrs. Jeffries said quietly. Regardless of how badly she needed information, her conscience could not let Mrs. Goodge's last remark pass without comment.

"But that's what they was, a savage mob," the cook argued. "And Colonel Seaward was badly wounded. He left the army and came back to England. That's when he was decorated by Her Majesty."

"When did this happen?"

"About ten or twelve years ago." Mrs. Goodge picked up the rolling pin. "But he's not one of those idle do-nothings. He's worked for the government ever since. I hear he's in line for a very important appointment."

"Indeed? What kind of an appointment?"

"Governor to one of them islands out in the Caribbean." She shook her head. "Sounds like one of them right nasty places. Hot, miserable and the people running around half-undressed. Makes a body wonder why anyone would want to go to such a place. But that's the kind of man Colonel

Seaward is, a real gentleman. Knows his duty. Never any scandal attached to his name, I can tell you that."

Mrs. Jeffries had no doubt that she could. "Is he married?"

"No. He's given his whole life to public service. If you ask me, I think the country needs more like him."

"Yes," Mrs. Jeffries replied softly, "I'm sure you do. Do you know anything about Catherine Leslie or Dr. Hightower?"

The cook's brows drew together. "I'm not sure. The names sound a bit familiar, but I can't think of anything right off. I'll let you know if I remember anything."

"Thank you, Mrs. Goodge. That'll be fine." Deep in thought, Mrs. Jeffries walked away. At the door, she stopped. "When is the announcement of Colonel Seaward's appointment expected to be made?"

"Why, I believe it's to be this week sometime. When Her Majesty returns from Balmoral."

"Good heavens, man. You've upset Mrs. Leslie terribly and I won't stand for it, do you hear? I don't care if you are the police, that doesn't give you the right to come barging in here and making ridiculous accusations." Dr. Sebastian Hightower paused to take a breath. "Furthermore—"

"Dr. Hightower," Inspector Witherspoon interrupted, "I assure you, sir, I did not mean to upset the lady, but this is a murder investigation. I've no idea why Mrs. Leslie became so distraught over a few simple questions. Questions, I might add, that everyone living on these gardens has had to answer."

He was getting annoyed. But drat it all, nothing had gone right today. He'd been on his way out to try and get to the Slocum solicitor when Mrs. Leslie's maid, Nanette, had popped up like a rabbit out of a hat and imperiously demanded that he return to the Leslie house.

He would have gone back there in any case, he thought defensively. But he certainly didn't like being summoned as if he were an errant schoolboy, and by none other than the arrogant Dr. Hightower. "And if you'll recall, sir, I didn't barge in here, you sent the maid over to ask me to come."

"Right, well." Hightower had the good grace to flush. "I thought it was important to get to the heart of this matter as soon as possible. Nanette told me that Mrs. Leslie fainted while you were questioning her this morning."

"That's correct. As I said, she became most distraught, as did the maid."

"Yes, well, that's the point I'm trying to make. Mrs. Leslie has a very high-strung and nervous disposition. She upsets easily. The least little thing sets her off, and I wouldn't want the police to place undue importance on a minor fainting spell."

"I see." Witherspoon didn't see in the least. What on earth was the man trying to tell him? That he wasn't supposed to question people in a murder case because they might faint! Ridiculous. "Dr. Hightower, I've placed no importance whatsoever on Mrs. Leslie's behavior this morning. Why it's a well-known fact that females frequently swoon."

"Good. I'm glad you understand."

"However," Witherspoon continued as though Hightower hadn't spoken. "Though I've no wish to distress either Mrs. Leslie or her maid any further, I will be asking them more questions. There are several unusual facts to this matter that must be clarified."

Dr. Hightower stared at him incredulously. "If you must ask your blasted questions, sir," he snapped, "then I suggest you direct them to me. I can assure you, Mrs. Leslie had absolutely nothing to do with Dr. Slocum's murder."

Witherspoon gazed at him thoughtfully. "You couldn't, by any chance, shed any light on what the maid was on about? She kept saying that Mrs. Leslie shouldn't lie to the police. That she must tell the truth. Do you know what she was talking about?"

"*Non!* 'E does not."

The inspector whirled around at the sound of the girl's voice and saw her standing by the door. "Then perhaps you'd care to tell me what you were talking about," he said.

She shrugged. "As I told you when we were walking over here, there ees nothing to say. I was upset. I thought you were going to arrest my mistress. The English polees, they are always arresting innocent people."

Witherspoon gazed at her pityingly. Poor child, she didn't know what she was talking about. But then what could one expect from the French? Why it was a well-known fact that anarchists, revolutionaries and even worse walked the streets of Paris without so much as a by-your-leave.

"But you said this morning," he continued, getting back to the matter at hand, "that Dr. Slocum threatened to tell lies about your mistress. Isn't that true?"

"You misunderstood me, Monsieur Inspector. I meant that I was afraid the polees would believe lies about my mistress. The British, they are always gossiping and making up tales."

"But you said . . ." Witherspoon broke off in confusion. Blast it, what all had the girl said? Something about a key, and yes, calling cards. "You stated that Dr. Slocum dropped two calling cards here on the day he died."

The girl glanced quickly at Hightower and then back at the inspector. But it was the doctor who answered.

"He did. But there was nothing unusual in that. Dr. Slocum was constantly trying to push himself upon his neighbors." He turned to the maid. "That'll be all, Nanette. Please go and sit with Mrs. Leslie. We'll call you if we need you."

Witherspoon waited until the girl had left. "So Dr. Slocum wasn't a welcome guest here?"

"No. Mrs. Leslie didn't like the man. Nor did anyone else."

Witherspoon racked his brain for another question. "You were, I believe, at Mrs. Crookshank's party this past Saturday?"

"Yes. Mrs. Crookshank is quite a forceful person. It's difficult to refuse her invitations. Besides, I like the lady. Despite her rather colorful way with words, she's a most charming and kindhearted woman."

"And why were you invited? You don't live on the gardens."

Hightower looked surprised by the question. "I was invited because I'm Mrs. Crookshank's physician as well as her friend."

"So you and Mrs. Leslie were both present when Mrs. Crookshank told the gardener to get rid of the poisonous mushrooms?" Witherspoon was sure he was on to something here.

"Yes. But the way Mrs. Crookshank bellows, I shouldn't be surprised if half of London heard her ranting and raving about those mushrooms." Hightower's eyes narrowed. "What are you trying to imply?"

"Why, nothing. I'm merely trying to ascertain how many people knew the mushrooms were there. That was how he was killed, you know."

Dr. Hightower stared at him incredulously for a moment. "Mushroom poisoning? Good Lord, man, you must be joking."

"I assure you, I'm not. How did you think he'd been killed?"

"I knew Slocum had been poisoned." Hightower's brows drew together. "But I didn't know it had anything to do with mushrooms. Are you sure?"

"Quite sure," Witherspoon said defensively. "Our police surgeon confirmed it."

"Did he do a postmortem examination? Was he absolutely sure about the cause of death?"

The inspector felt his hackles rising. "Really, Doctor. Of course I'm sure. We are very thorough at Scotland Yard, certainly capable of ascertaining the correct cause of death."

Dr. Hightower stared at him silently.

After a few moments, Witherspoon pulled out his watch and checked the time. "I really must be off," he said. "I'll have to come back and finish questioning Mrs. Leslie tomorrow."

"As her physician, I'd like to be present when you do."

Witherspoon wasn't sure he liked that, but he couldn't think of any legal grounds upon which to object. "As you wish, sir. Until tomorrow."

It started to rain right after lunch, and Mrs. Jeffries decided to put off her return to the Slocum house till the next morning. Trudging about in the wet would only hamper her search for clues.

After tea, she went up to her sitting room at the top of the house and started to think in earnest about the murder of Bartholomew Slocum.

He was a nasty little man, she decided, taking a seat by the window and staring down at the street below. Slocum was miserly with tradespeople, miserable to his servants and refused to treat patients who couldn't pay. But none of that added up to a reasonably good motive for murder. Or did it? She leaned back in the chair, closed her eyes and let her mind wander.

If Slocum had been murdered in a fit of rage, perhaps what she'd learned of his character could be of some use. But he hadn't been killed on the spur of the moment. He hadn't been stabbed by a servant driven to his or her limit of endurance, and he hadn't been attacked suddenly by a shopkeeper or a rejected patient because of his mean and miserly ways.

No, she thought, this crime had been carefully and meticulously planned. Someone had deliberately slipped a poisoned mushroom into his soup bowl. Someone had known he was going to be alone in the house and unable to summon help. Someone had known his habits and his customs. Someone who wanted him dead had known the servants were going to be gone and that his surgery would be closed. And that someone had then seized the opportunity to kill him. She didn't for a minute think that person was a middle-aged, frightened cook either.

No. Whoever had done the deed was cool, calculating and desperate.

"Good evening, sir," Mrs. Jeffries reached for Inspector Witherspoon's bowler hat. "I hope you've had a successful day."

"Well, it's actually been quite a dreadful day," he answered with a weary smile. "But I think I've learned some important facts about the case, so I suppose it's been worth it. Shall we have a glass of sherry before dinner? I daresay I could use a bit of warming up."

"I've got you a glass poured," she said, following him down the hall and into the drawing room. She handed him a glass and picked up the one she'd poured for herself.

He took a sip of his drink. "I questioned the solicitor today. Chap was as you'd expect, tight-lipped and well . . . not very accomodating. Naturally, when I impressed upon him how grave the situation was, he was a bit more forthcoming."

"I presume he told you the terms of Dr. Slocum's will?"

"Yes, and very interesting it was too. Slocum was going to leave his estate to his nephew, Joshua Slocum. But a few weeks ago, he suddenly changed his mind."

Her eyes widened in surprise. "Really."

"Oh yes. According to Mr. Carp, the solicitor. Slocum asked him to come round because he wanted to alter his will. This was two weeks ago. Mr. Carp told us that Slocum gave him instructions to change the will completely. Instead of leaving the bulk of his estate to his nephew, he'd decided to use his money in quite a different manner."

"He was leaving everything to someone else?" Mrs. Jeffries asked.

Witherspoon smiled slightly. "Not quite. You see Slocum had a decidedly high opinion of himself. He was going to build a memorial to himself after he was dead. Every penny was to be used to endow a wing in his name at the hospital in Chelmsford. Oh yes, and he also left instructions that they had to put up a statue to him as well. So you see, there's absolutely no doubt about it now. The new will is the key to the murder. Effie Beals killed him for the hundred pounds he left her in his old will."

"So he had left bequests to the servants in his old will," Mrs. Jeffries mused. "But if he made a new will, why would the cook murder him now?"

Witherspoon smiled. "Simple. Mr. Carp came down with gout and that delayed the drafting of the new will. Until it was signed and properly witnessed, the old will was still the legal document for the dispersion of the Slocum estate. Joshua Slocum is still the heir and Mrs. Effie Beals will get her hundred pounds—well, she would if she wasn't going to be arrested for Dr. Slocum's murder, that is."

"But how did she know Slocum had left her any money?" Mrs. Jeffries asked. "Surely he didn't tell her."

"Of course he didn't. But unfortunately one of the witnesses did," Witherspoon explained. "I'm afraid Mrs. Melcher called in for a sleeping potion and Slocum made the mistake of asking her to sign as witness to the will. She obliged and then promptly told the whole neighborhood what she'd seen."

"And what did she see?" Mrs. Jeffries asked. She could see the hangman's noose edging closer to Effie Beal's neck, and she didn't like it one bit.

"The bequests to the servants." Witherspoon said sadly. "The woman could read, and those particular items were on the last page. Her signature was just below it."

"I see. Did he leave the other servants the same amount?"

The inspector shook his head. "Only the butler. He got a hundred too, the maids and the footmen were each given twenty-five. But Effie Beals is the only one with the motive and the opportunity. All the rest of the household had already gone when she served his lunch to him."

As a motive, Mrs. Jeffries thought it was fairly weak.

"But surely, killing Dr. Slocum would be a bit like killing the goose that laid the golden egg," she said. "After all, he was her employer—once he was dead, she'd be out of work."

"Well, yes," the inspector mumbled with a puzzled frown, "but a hundred pounds is a lot of money to someone like her. She doesn't strike me as being an overly intelligent woman. I suspect she acted on the spur of the moment without thinking of the possible future consequences of her actions. So many of that class of people live only for today. They don't stop to consider what might happen tomorrow."

Mrs. Jeffries let that ridiculous statement pass without comment. Witherspoon, despite his good heart, wasn't immune to the prejudices and beliefs of his class. But she would hardly think that killing someone with a poisoned mushroom was a spur-of-the-moment act. They had to be picked and probably pressed or pulped as well. She'd just have to work harder to prove that Effie Beals hadn't done it.

"Yes, Inspector," she replied, "I expect you're correct. By the way, I thought I saw Inspector Nivens come in as I left."

"How observant you are," Witherspoon exclaimed. "The fellow dropped by to ask if he could lend a hand in the Slocum matter. He's already solved that robbery in Holland Park. Generous of him, wasn't it? He even offered to escort the maid back to the Leslie house and question Dr. Hightower for me, but naturally, I told him I'd have to do that. And I'm jolly glad I did too. Do you know, that Hightower fellow actually had the gall to hint that our police surgeon was mistaken about the cause of death?" Witherspoon set his glass down with a loud thunk. "Can't imagine what Nivens would have made of that. He'd have probably lost his temper. Yes, yes, it's a good thing I took care of that matter—"

"Inspector, please," Mrs. Jeffries interrupted. "You're getting ahead of yourself." She paused and gave him a guileless smile. "Now, why don't you tell me all about your visit to the Leslie house?"

She listened patiently as Witherspoon gave her the details of both his first and second visits to the Leslie household.

"But you know, Mrs. Jeffries," he said as he concluded the narrative, "going over it again leads me to believe there's there's something deucedly strange going on there. Don't you think so? I mean, I know I couldn't have been mistaken about the maid's statement this morning. Yet this afternoon, she'd completely changed her story. Makes one think, doesn't it?"

"Then you're not absolutely convinced Effie Beals is guilty?" she asked cautiously. "Do you think perhaps you ought to investigate just a bit more? Especially about the matter of the calling cards."

"That's the puzzle," he muttered. "Perhaps I should. The evidence points to the cook, but somehow, I get the feeling there's more to this case than meets the eye. Too many loose ends, that's what it is. And you know how I hate loose ends."

"Then you'll continue the investigation?"

"Oh yes," he exclaimed. "My conscience would torment me horribly if I arrested the woman now. I'm almost positive she did it, but until a few other questions are settled to my satisfaction, I won't rest."

"I'm delighted to hear you say that," Mrs. Jeffries said earnestly. "And what other loose ends are troubling you?"

"The house being empty was one worry, but I think I've solved that to my satisfaction."

"Do tell," she coaxed. "You know I so love hearing how you've arrived at your conclusions."

His chest swelled and he sat straighter. "Ah yes, my conclusions. First of all, the house was empty because he'd given the staff the day off. That in and of itself was unusual, but upon serious questioning of the servants, I found it wasn't the first time it had happened."

She bit her tongue to keep from telling him they already knew that.

"But the important question," he continued, "was determining whether or not the house being empty had any connection with the doctor's death. It didn't."

Mrs. Jeffries stared at him in amazement. "How did you deduce that?"

"The calling cards. Dr. Slocum had sent his calling card to several of his neighbors the day before. Well, it's perfectly obvious."

"What is?" Her jaw was beginning to ache with the effort it took to keep a pleasant smile on her face.

"Dr. Slocum," he explained, smiling at her benevolently, "was not a very popular man. But he never stopped trying to become better acquainted with his neighbors. From what we've learned of his actions in the twenty-four hours before he died, I've concluded that he took his calling card around hoping one of his neighbors would return the favor and drop by on the afternoon of his death. Not only did he go round with his card, but he also ordered the butler to bring up a case of his best French wine. Naturally, if a guest dropped by, he wanted to be able to offer them refreshment."

"But if he were expecting *guests*," she said, deliberately stressing the last word, "wouldn't he have made sure that at least the maid and butler were on hand to serve them?"

"Not necessarily. If he were expecting a gentleman to come, he could easily pour a glass of wine."

"But you know that he sent a card to Mrs. Leslie," Mrs. Jeffries said. "She's a lady. He'd have kept at least a maid in attendance if he were expecting her."

"I think not, Mrs. Jeffries," Witherspoon said, shifting uncomfortably. "Slocum was a man of the world . . ." He paused and coughed lightly as a blush crept up his cheeks. "Mrs. Leslie is a very beautiful woman. I suspect he deliberately got rid of the servants so he could be alone with her."

CHAPTER 7

Betsy popped her head into the drawing room and announced that dinner was served, so Mrs. Jeffries had to wait until the inspector was settled at the dining table before she could continue her questions.

"Are you suggesting Dr. Slocum was arranging an assignation of a romantic nature, then?" Mrs. Jeffries asked briskly as the inspector picked up his fork.

The fork halted halfway to Witherspoon's mouth. He'd just remembered the second card, the one for Dr. Hightower.

"Well, not exactly," he hedged. "You see, when he dropped the card off for Mrs. Leslie, he also left one for Dr. Hightower." He looked down at his steak and kidney pudding to hide his confusion. "But I'm sure his taking the cards around hadn't anything to do with his murder. Dr. Slocum was merely trying to become better acquainted with his neighbors. Yes, that's what the fellow was doing. I'm sure of it. The cards are nothing more than a coincidence. Nothing to do with the case at all."

Mrs. Jeffries stared at him, debating whether or not to tell him about the calling card left at Colonel Seaward's. Seeing the confusion in the inspector's eyes, she decided to say nothing for the moment. Those cards were important, but she wasn't sure precisely what they meant. But she would find out, and she thought she knew exactly how to do it.

"It's rather sad, isn't it?" she remarked with a theatrical sigh.

"What is?"

"The way the poor man was continually trying to establish friendships with his neighbors. I suppose he wasn't particularly gifted at getting others to like him all that much." She turned her head and sniffed. "And then he was murdered. It's heartbreaking."

"Dear, dear, Mrs. Jeffries," the inspector said, leaning forward and patting her hand. "Don't distress yourself so. Dr. Slocum wasn't in the habit of going around with his hat in hand begging for friendship. Why, Keating's told us he only went out to call once every quarter or so."

She turned and gave him a brilliant smile. "I'm so glad to hear that. It's dreadful thinking of that poor man all alone, friendless and desperate for companionship."

"You're much too kindhearted, Mrs. Jeffries. Don't waste your sympathy on Dr. Slocum. By all accounts, he was a perfectly happy man living his life entirely as he wished."

"That is good to hear." For effect, she paused momentarily and piously gazed down at her folded hands. Then she suddenly straightened and lifted her chin to meet Witherspoon's gaze. "Inspector," she said breathlessly, "you really are a sly one, aren't you?"

Witherspoon gaped at her from behind a forkful of mashed potato he was trying to get to his mouth. "Pardon?"

"Why, of course you are," she exclaimed. "But that's all right, you can play the innocent with me. I know precisely how that mind of yours works, and I know you won't be so cruel as to keep me in the dark. I shall expect a full accounting tomorrow at dinner." She laughed merrily. "Oh my, you are a clever man."

Witherspoon put the bite of potato back on his plate. "Yes, I suppose I am." He gave a deprecatory laugh. "But then it's no use trying to hide my methods from you, is it?" He paused and cleared his throat. "Just for the sake of argument, Mrs. Jeffries, what do you think I'm going to do tomorrow?" He leaned forward, eyeing her the way a dog does a meaty bone.

Mrs. Jeffries didn't like tormenting her kindly employer. She'd hoped he'd grasp her meaning without her having actually to come right out and say it, but he obviously wasn't going to. She cocked her head to one side and smiled conspiratorially. "You're going to find out if Dr. Slocum's calling upon his neighbors ever coincided with his unexpectedly giving the servants the day off."

Witherspoon blinked several times and then sat back, a bemused expression on his face. "What a good idea," he murmured. He sat up taller in his chair. "Of course it's a good idea," he exclaimed in a stronger tone of voice, "and that's precisely what I was planning on doing."

Satisfied, Mrs. Jeffries nodded. She heard the rustle of a starched apron and glanced at the door. Betsy was standing in the hall, directly behind the inspector and jerking her chin frantically toward the kitchen.

"If you'll excuse me, Inspector," she said, rising quickly and hurrying toward the door. "I must see to your coffee."

Betsy motioned her down to the end of the hallway.

"We've got a message from Smythe," she whispered excitedly. "A rag and bone man just brung it—he says Smythe says to say he's hot on the trail, but he don't say on whose trail or why. He says not to worry, he'll be back in a day or so."

"Thank goodness we've finally heard from him," Mrs. Jeffries replied. "I don't mind admitting I was getting alarmed. Smythe is an admirable man and well able to take care of himself, but even so, it's been two days."

"But what does it mean? That old rag and bone man won't tell us anything else. He didn't say where Smythe was or anythin' useful. He's just sittin' downstairs stuffin' in the last of Mrs. Goodge's treacle tarts."

Most housemaids would rather die than admit to their employer or their employer's representative that the cook was feeding someone other than a member of the family or a guest. But Betsy knew that she was safe in telling the housekeeper. Their household wasn't like anyone else's, and that was all there was to it. Mrs. Jeffries practically encouraged such behavior. And after watching the way Mrs. Goodge got the old man to talking, Betsy was beginning to suspect she knew why too. But she'd keep that little tidbit to herself. It was too good to pass on now. Yet someday, when Mrs. Jeffries really needed proof of how good her detectin' skills was gettin', she'd reveal exactly how their snobbish old cook knew what was going on in this town without ever leaving the kitchen.

"Don't fret about Smythe, Betsy," Mrs. Jeffries soothed, "I think I know what he's doing. But I do wish he'd come back soon. There's a matter or two I'd like him to look into."

Betsy's blue eyes sparkled like dewdrops in the sun. "I can look into it for ya," she blurted. "I can find out anything Smythe can. Just give a us chance. 'E's not 'ere and I am, and there's no tellin' when 'e'll be back. Come on, Mrs. J, please. Let me 'ave a go at it."

She drops her h's completely when she's excited, Mrs. Jeffries thought idly as she stared into the girl's eager face. "But you don't even know what it is I want you to do."

"That's all right; whatever it is, I'm willin'."

Mrs. Jeffries silently debated the issue and then made her decision. Betsy was right; she was here and Smythe wasn't. "All right. Here's what I want you to do. Tomorrow, you'll have to go back to Knightsbridge. We need to know several things. One, find out anything you can about the butler. When I spoke to him yesterday, he seemed to think I was there to 'tell tales' of some sort or another. See if you can pick up any gossip about his activities. Also, try and make the acquaintance of someone from the Slocum household—a housemaid or a footman, if you can. The Leslie maid was going on about a key the doctor always carried. See if you can get any information about that."

Betsy nodded gravely. "That shouldn't be too hard. I think I can do it."

"I know you can," Mrs. Jeffries said earnestly. She'd often observed that people generally lived up to whatever expectations they had of themselves. Building someone's self-confidence did a lot more good in getting the best results out of people than making them feel as if they couldn't do anything right. "I have complete faith in you, Betsy. But for goodness' sakes, be careful."

The next morning, Mrs. Jeffries waited until Inspector Witherspoon had left before donning her hat and cloak. She caught a hansom on Holland Park Road because she was in a hurry to get to Knightsbridge. If she were lucky, one of the side gates leading into the communal garden would still be unlocked. Frequently, lazy groundskeepers unlocked the gates early in the mornings so they wouldn't be bothered having to let tradespeople and delivery men in and out.

As the hansom clopped briskly toward Dr. Slocum's residence, Mrs. Jeffries thought carefully of how to approach Effie Beals. By the time the horses had stopped on the side street, near the gate, she'd made up her mind.

Mrs. Jeffries paid the driver, tipped him handsomely and then slipped through the unlocked (just as she'd thought) gate. She stopped inside and slowly looked around. The gardens were an elongated octagon. Along the center strip was a spacious expanse of grass dotted here and there with tall, sheltering oak trees. Beside the grass and circling the perimeter of the octagon was a ten-foot strip of space filled with a variety of plants, flowers and greenery, Obviously, each household had the right to plant whatever they liked in the space adjacent to their property. Behind some houses there were high shrubs, while others had neatly laid rows of flowers and shrubs. She noticed that the Seaward house occupied all the room at the far end of the octagon and that the strip of garden there was virtually a jungle. The shrubs and plants were so thick and high one could probably get lost in them. The foliage extended virtually all the way to the Slocum house.

She raised her hand to shade her eyes against the sunlight as she studied the area. Each house had one thing in common, she thought. A path leading from a recessed area behind the houses through their bits of private garden onto the main garden. As she walked toward the Slocum house, she noticed that each individual path went down a set of stone stairs onto a flat terrace about ten feet by ten feet.

Intent upon reaching her goal, she didn't hear the shuffle of footsteps coming up behind her.

"Yoo-hoo," screeched a familiar flat twang.

Mrs. Jeffries started and whirled. Luty Belle Crookshank, dressed in a garish green dress, trimmed with gold on the cuffs and collars, stood grinning at her.

"It's Mrs. Jeffries, ain't it?" said Luty Belle. "Well, I sure am glad to see you. Ever since ol' Slocum went and got himself done in, this place has been like a ghost town. You'd think the man died of the pox, the way folks has been avoiding coming out here."

Mrs. Jeffries edged closer to the Slocum terrace. She had a feeling that if she started a conversation with Luty Belle, she'd be there half the day. And she had so much to do. "Good morning, Mrs. Crookshank," she said politely, as she continued moving toward the Slocum house.

"Told you to call me Luty Belle. Purty day, ain't it?" Luty Belle came after her. "Would you like to have a cuppa tea?"

"Er, no thank you, Luty Belle. I'm in rather a hurry this morning."

"That's the problem with folks these days," Luty Belle complained. "Always in a dang-blasted hurry to get somewhere. Where you headed? Over to the Slocum house?"

"Yes, as a matter of fact, I am."

"Good, then you can take a message to them fatheaded lawmen for me. Been trying to git one of them to stand still so's I could tell for the past two days now, but every time they see me coming, they take off like the hounds of hell was chasin' 'em."

Mrs. Jeffries stopped dead. "Do you have some information about Dr. Slocum's murder?"

"Murder? If'n what I heard is true there might not even have been a murder." Luty Belle cackled.

"What are you talking about?"

"Dead eyes. That's what they're saying killed him, inn't that so?"

"Yes," Mrs. Jeffries replied. "That's correct. Do you have a reason to believe otherwise?"

Luty Belle cocked her head to one side. "Sure do. You see, I knows how dead eyes kill, and the only ways Slocum could have died from eatin' one was if he ate it a good four days earlier than the day he died. Dead eyes don't kill you quick, you see. They makes you real sick and then it looks like you're gittin' well, but then you take a turn for the worse and finally go a few days later. But it takes at least four days and if'n what I heard was right, they're saying the doctor ate the danged thing for lunch and then keeled over right away." Luty Belle shook her head. "But that weren't the way it happened. Couldn't be, and I should know."

Mrs. Jeffries was utterly stunned. Surely the police surgeon couldn't make a mistake. Surely this old woman was wrong. "How do you know?" she finally asked.

" 'Cause I've seen folks die that way," she said impatiently. "What do you think I'm doin', making up tales just for my own entertainment? Back in '53 I nursed two miners who'd eated dead eyes. It was a bad year; people was starvin' 'cause the snow was so bad no supplies could get through. As soon as some of the snow melted, these two miners went mushroomin'; they was that hungry. My Archie and I we took 'em in when they got sick, and I nursed 'em. Nells Bells," Luty Belle banged her cane against the ground. "It took one of them four days to go and the other one almost a week. So take my word for it, Slocum didn't die in two hours from eatin' no poisoned mushroom."

Mrs. Jeffries studied the old woman's face. She could see from the determined glint in Luty Belle's eyes that she was telling the truth. Maybe the police surgeon had made a mistake. "Luty Belle," she said slowly. "If you're right . . ."

"Course I'm right." Luty Belle snorted. "And from what I hears, they're gittin' ready to arrest Slocum's cook. Stupid lawmen, same the world over, always taking the easy way out—"

"Would you like to prevent a gross miscarriage of justice?" Mrs. Jeffries interrupted.

Luty Belle stared at her warily. "I reckon. Don't want to see someone that's innocent strung up like a side of beef. What do you think I should do?"

Suddenly inspired, Mrs. Jeffries said, "You've got to find Inspector Witherspoon and tell him everything you've told me." She paused, trying to remember precisely where Witherspoon said he might be this morning. There were several places. Quickly, she rattled the list off to Luty Belle.

"And don't let one of his underlings put you off," she finished. "You've got to make sure Inspector Witherspoon understands everything you've told me."

"Reckons traipin' round London lookin' for this copper beats sittin' in that empty old mausoleum of a house o' mine," Luty said cheerfully as she turned to go.

"Oh and Luty Belle," Mrs. Jeffries called. The woman stopped and gazed at her inquiringly. "It would be best if you didn't mention our little chat to the inspector."

The Slocum terrace was put to practical use. Outside the kitchen door there was a long table with several baskets of vegetables sitting on it. Mrs. Jeffries hurried past them and marched boldly up to the kitchen door. She rapped her knuckles imperiously against the wood.

The door opened about two inches, and a pair of worried eyes glared at her suspiciously from within. "Yes, what do you want?"

"Mrs. Effie Beals?"

The door closed to an inch. "Who wants to know?"

"Mrs. Beals, I've come to help you." Mrs. Jeffries surreptitiously wedged her toe close to the door.

"Help," snorted the woman. "We don't need no help here. The solicitor didn't say he was sending anyone round, so you've got no business here." She jerked the door open wider as a forerunner to slamming it shut, but Mrs. Jeffries was too quick for her and managed to get her heavily booted foot inside.

"You don't understand," Mrs. Jeffries said firmly. "I haven't come to help you in the kitchen, I've come to help you keep from being arrested for a murder you didn't commit."

The suspicious eyes widened in fright, and Effie Beals stared at her as if she'd seen a ghost. For a long moment, the two women took each other's measure. Finally, the door opened fully and the cook jerked her chin once in the direction of the house. Mrs. Jeffries took that to mean she was welcome to come inside.

"Thank you, Mrs. Beals," she said politely as she stepped inside. "I realize this is most irregular, but I assure you, you've nothing to fear from me."

"Are you from the police?" Effie asked as she moved slowly down the hallway.

"No."

"Then why are you here?"

They came into the servants' hall. "If it's no trouble, I could do with a cup of tea," she said matter-of-factly. People always spoke more easily over a nice hot cuppa, she thought.

The cook stared at her for a moment. "I've just made a pot; nothing much else to do now, but drink tea. Now that he's dead, we just have simple meals down here. Between the ruddy police and that ferret of a solicitor, we're all stuck here until this misery's done."

By that, Mrs. Jeffries assumed she was referring to the investigation of Slocum's murder. She took a seat at the table and waited while Effie Beals poured two cups of tea, found a tin of sugar and a pitcher of cream, placed the whole lot on a tray and came to join her.

The cook's apron was wrinkled, her eyes were red, and as she poured the tea, Mrs. Jeffries saw her hands shaking.

"Mrs. Beals," she said softly, "I really have come to help you."

"How can you help me?" the woman wailed. Tears slipped down her cheeks, and she hung her head. "No one can help me. He's dead and they think I killed him. Besides, why should you care? And you never told me what you was doing here, neither."

"My name is Hepzibah Jeffries and I'm Inspector Witherspoon's housekeeper." There was a strangled gasp from Effie Beals, but Mrs. Jeffries resolutely ignored it. "I've come here because, well, I'm quite astute at solving mysteries and I've realized you couldn't possibly have killed Bartholomew Slocum."

Another strangled gasp, and Effie Beal's mouth gaped open like a flounder's. Mrs. Jeffries held up her hand for silence.

"Like you, I'm in domestic service. However, I'm reasonably intelligent, very observant, and more importantly, I can think. If you will answer my questions honestly and quickly, we may just be able to keep a hangman from stretching your neck."

She'd deliberately used the brutal words to shock the woman and gain her cooperation. Time was running out. She didn't have the luxury of winning Effie Beal's confidence with her usual patience and tact.

Effie sniffed and brushed at an escaping tear. "You think I'm innocent?"

"I'm certain of it." After meeting the cook face-to-face, Mrs. Jeffries was positive she wasn't guilty. After what Luty Belle had told her, she didn't know precisely what to think. But she did know that Slocum's murder, if it had been murder, was carefully and meticulously planned.

Effie Beals was an emotional woman. Only a great actress could fake this level of distress. If this weeping woman were going to kill someone, she'd do it in a frenzy of rage and quite probably in front of a dozen witnesses!

Effie bowed her head and sobbed quietly into her apron. Mrs. Jeffries waited patiently, knowing the woman needed a few moments to work the fear out of her system.

With a final shudder, she brought herself under control, wiped her cheeks and lifted her head. "Let's get on with them questions of yours," she said, giving Mrs. Jeffries a watery smile. "Do you want me to tell what happened that day?"

"No, that won't be necessary. I know the sequence of events. You've got to tell me *why* someone would want to murder Bartholomew Slocum."

"Why? That's simple enough," she replied with a snort. "He's a blackmailer."

"How do you know that?" Mrs. Jeffries found that she wasn't in the least surprised.

"Because he was blackmailin' me." Effie lifted her chin. "You don't think I'm workin 'ere by choice, do you? The old bastard forced me to come here. And it's such a bleedin' waste too. He didn't appreciate fine cooking. The man had a palate like a billy goat, wouldn't know good food if he was buried in it up to his arse."

"His palate, or lack of it, isn't pertinent right now," Mrs. Jeffries said firmly, excusing the vulgarity. "But you must tell me why he was blackmailing you."

Effie dropped her eyes and stared at the toe of her scuffed black shoe. "Do you have to know that?"

"Yes, I'm afraid I do."

The cook raised her chin, and her eyes were awash with fresh tears. "All right then, I'm trustin' that what I'm going to tell you will go no farther. It's not myself I'm worryin' about," she said quickly, "it's someone else, someone very dear to me."

Mrs. Jeffries reached over and patted her arm. "Believe me, Mrs. Beals," she said softly, "I'll do everything in my power to insure that innocent people aren't ruined because of this murder. But I can't give you any promises. If the information you're going to give me will save you from the gallows, I'll certainly use it."

"Fair enough." She took a deep breath and focused her gaze on the far wall. "Ten years ago I was the cook at the country house of a very important family, aristocrats. I was a widow and it was a fine position because they let me keep my daughter with me." She broke off and smiled sadly. "Abigail was fourteen and the prettiest child you ever saw. But it seems that the young master of the house thought she was pretty too, because he seduced her, and him a grown man who should have known better. He got her . . . ," her voice faltered and she bit her lip, "with child."

"I'm so very sorry," Mrs. Jeffries said quietly.

Effie nodded, and her hands balled into fists. "I confronted the family and told them what their son had done. I expected them to own up to it, to help me daughter. For goodness' sakes, she weren't but a child." She gave a bitter laugh. Mrs. Jeffries was fairly certain she could guess the rest of the tale. "But they sacked me and threw us both out. But I weren't too scared. I'd saved me wages, and I knew I could get another position. I took me girl to London. The son, maybe having a bit more of a conscience than his father, gave me a reference to the London house of the Duke of Bedford. So I had me employment, but I couldn't keep me girl with me, not in her condition. I got her rooms with a respectable woman in Hammersmith and paid the lady to keep an eye on her."

"And Dr. Slocum delivered the baby?" Mrs. Jeffries asked.

"No, when she was five months along, she lost it. She were bleedin' so bad I thought for sure she'd die, so I sent the landlady for the doctor. It was Slocum."

"And he managed to save your daughter's life."

"Yes, he saved her, but he charged us a pretty penny, I can tell you that, not that I minded payin'," Effie explained earnestly, "but I didn't like his manner. He was wicked, he was. Filled her with some damned potion that made her ramble on and on. And he was askin' her questions, gettin' her to own up to who the father was and pokin' his nose in where it didn't belong. I soon put a stop to that bit o' meanness, I did. Paid the man an extra guinea to shut his mouth." She laughed harshly. "The old miser took it and left. I'd hope that we was shut of him, then. But we wasn't."

"Is that when he started the blackmail?"

"No, that didn't start for another five years."

"Five years?" Mrs. Jeffries stared at her curiously.

"When my daughter was nineteen she got engaged to a right nice young gentleman. His family owned a draper's shop here in London, and they was going to open another one in Chelmsford." She shook her head sadly. "I don't know how that old goat found out, it weren't in the papers or anything. But one day I got a note telling me to come round here to see him on my day off. Well, what could I do? I came round, and old Slocum told me if I wanted my daughter to marry, I'd better give in my notice to the duke and come work for him. If I didn't, he threatened to tell Abigail's fiancé about what had happened."

"I take it your daughter didn't share that confidence with her intended?"

"Would you?"

"No," Mrs. Jeffries said thoughtfully, "I probably wouldn't." It was her experience that men were exceedingly narrow-minded about some things. "So Slocum didn't blackmail you for money, he wanted you to work here, is that right?"

"That's right. You see, I'd begun to make a real name for meself with me cooking. Slocum didn't care none about the food, though, he just wanted the appearance of having one of the best cooks in London in his household. And not only that, the old miser cut my wages when I came here. I was making a full wage with the duke, seventy pounds a quarter. Slocum cut me to sixty pounds a quarter."

"Did your daughter know you were being blackmailed?"

Effie's eyes narrowed suspiciously at this question. "Abigail didn't have anything to do with Slocum's death," she said quickly. "She was at home the day he was killed."

"I'm not accusing your daughter of murder," Mrs. Jeffries replied patiently. "I merely want to know if she knew you were being blackmailed. Surely she asked you why you left the Duke of Bedford to come to work for a common doctor."

Effie glanced down at her hands. "She didn't know until a few weeks ago," she muttered sullenly. "When I left the Bedford house, I'd told her I was tired of working so hard and that all those fancy dinners were gettin' to be too much for me. I told her I needed a quieter life. She believed me for a while, but finally, I think she guessed I weren't here by choice."

"What prompted you to tell her the truth?"

"Last month Abigail told me she and Neville, that's her husband, were emigrating to Australia. She wanted me to come with 'em. I told her I couldn't—that Slocum probably wouldn't let me. If I left his employment, he'd tell Nev about her."

"What was her reaction?"

Effie smiled broadly. "She said she'd already told Nev everything and he didn't care. Told her he loved her no matter what, that she was his wife and they could have a good life in Australia. I was right proud of her. Nev's a good lad, and I know he loves her."

"So Dr. Slocum wouldn't have been able to blackmail you anymore," Mrs. Jeffries said thoughtfully.

"That's right. It done me heart good to tell that old bastard I was leavin'. That's why I stayed after the others had already gone—I give him my notice, told him I was going to Australia with my daughter and her husband and there weren't nothing he could do about it."

"How did Dr. Slocum take that news?" Mrs. Jeffries was genuinely curious.

"He was furious. That's what we had the row about. He ranted and raved and had a right fit over it."

"Did you know the doctor had left you a hundred pounds in his will?" Mrs. Jeffries watched the cook carefully, but Effie met her gaze squarely.

"Yes, I knew. But that didn't make no difference; he was changin' his will anyway. Keating told us that. And I didn't want the old bastard's blood money anyways. Why should I? I've saved me wages for years."

"Keating told everyone in the household that Slocum was changing his will?" Mrs. Jeffries asked.

The cook nodded. "Yes, but it don't make no difference, they still think I done it." She began wringing her hands together as a fresh batch of tears rolled down her cheeks. "And now look at me. They's goin' to arrest me for murder. I'm not goin' to Australia, I'm goin' to hang."

Mrs. Jeffries grasped her firmly by the shoulders and shook her lightly. "Nonsense. You aren't going to hang. Mark my words, you'll be sailing with your daughter and son-in-law to a new life in Australia. But you'll have to help me save you."

Effied sniffed. "How? What can I do?"

"The first thing is to tell Inspector Witherspoon the truth. Once he knows that Slocum was blackmailing you, he'll start looking for other victims of the man's greed."

"Oh no," Effie wailed, "I couldn't do that. Maybe he won't find anyone but me."

"But you said that Slocum was a blackmailer. I presume that means he was blackmailing others as well."

"He was. But he was careful. I don't know who else he had his hooks into. I can't help you there. If the police find out he was blackmailin' me and they don't find no one else, that'll put the noose around my neck as sure as the sun rises on Monday morning."

Mrs. Jeffries realized that the woman had a point. The key to finding the murderer was in finding the other victims. But that might not be easy.

"All right," she agreed, "for right now, we'll keep this between us."

"Thank you, ma'am."

"Now, I want you to think. On the day of the murder, did you see anyone hanging about outside in the garden?" Mrs. Jeffries was fishing for any and all information she could find.

Effie's brows knotted in concentration. "Well, I saw that French maid of Mrs. Leslie's walking past with one of the gardeners when I was out getting the vegetables from the table. And Colonel Seaward went past right after that. But there weren't nothing strange about either of them. The maid was always making eyes at the gardener, and the colonel took a walk every morning."

"You saw Colonel Seaward that morning? Are you sure?"

"Yes, course I'm sure. I was just gettin' the mushrooms for the soup. It were about ten o'clock that mornin'. I saw him and that maid about the same time, but they was goin' in different directions."

Mrs. Jeffries frowned. "Was there anything else odd about that day? Anything, anything at all? Think, Mrs. Beals. Think hard."

"Well," she answered slowly, "there was one thing that puzzled me. But when I tried to tell the police, they weren't interested."

"What was that?"

"It was that Dr. Hightower findin' the body. He said he was callin' round to visit Dr. Slocum, but I don't think that's true."

"Really? Why?"

"Because he'd never have called around here by choice. He and Slocum hated each other."

CHAPTER 8

"Gracious, how on earth do you know that?" Mrs. Jeffries asked.

"Because I heard them fighting. Dr. Hightower claimed if he had anything to do with it, he'd see to it that Dr. Slocum never touched another patient for the rest of his life." Effie smiled smugly. "Now that don't sound like they was good friends, does it?"

"Apparently not."

"Mind you, I'm not surprised, despite this fancy house and all his rich patients, I don't think old Slocum was much of a doctor."

"Yet he saved your daughter," Mrs. Jeffries reminded her.

"He saved her all right," Effie said thoughtfully, "but I think any doctor could have done the same."

This was the second time Mrs. Jeffries had heard that Slocum wasn't a particularly good physician. She wondered if it were true. It hadn't really seemed likely to her the murderer could be a disgruntled patient, but perhaps she should reconsider.

"Mrs. Beals. Tell me how you came to overhear Dr. Slocum having words with Dr. Hightower."

"Well, it was one of them times when he'd unexpectedly given us the day off. I couldn't go to Abigail's because she and Nev had gone up to Yorkshire to see his Gran."

"How long ago was this?"

"I think it was about six months ago. It were one of them cold, wet, nasty days, and Slocum came trottin' in, ordering us out o' the house like he were doin' us a big favor. But who wants to leave a nice warm house on a day like that? I didn't. But he insisted we leave, so I didn't have much choice. I waited till the others had gone off and then nipped back through the garden. There weren't no one around, and I was thinking I'd just slip into my room and have a rest."

Her voice dropped dramatically. "That was when I heard 'em. They was upstairs, having a right go at each other."

"Slocum and Hightower? You're sure of that?"

"Yes." She nodded eagerly. "Hightower was shouting that Slocum weren't fit to doctor a horse and that if he ever touched her again, he'd have his license."

"Her? Did you hear the name of the lady they were arguing about?"

"I didn't hear him say it, but I reckon it must have been that Mrs. Leslie from across the garden. She used to be one of Dr. Slocum's patients. She quit coming to him when she and Dr. Hightower became friendly like."

"She was one of Slocum's patients? Are you sure?"

"I'm sure. He was treatin' her for some kind of nerve sickness."

"When did she stop seeing Slocum?"

"About two years ago," Effie said cautiously. "But anyways, it had to be her. Hightower's always hanging about over there. And that day, he and Slocum was arguin' loud enough to wake the dead. Just before Hightower left, I heard him threaten Dr. Slocum."

Mrs. Jeffries said nothing for a moment. She stared into space, her hands neatly folded in her lap and her eyes narrowed in concentration. She was sure that Inspector Witherspoon had told her that Mrs. Leslie denied ever being one of Slocum's patients.

"Mrs. Beals," she said slowly, "I want you to think carefully before you answer. Did you actually hear Dr.

Hightower threaten to kill Dr. Slocum? Did you actually hear him say so in the Queen's English—did you hear the words?"

Effie shifted nervously in her chair, her eyes darting furtively around the room. "Not exactly," she admitted, "but I'm sure that's what he meant."

"What were the exact words?" Mrs. Jeffries asked softly.

"He said, 'If you go near her again, I'll see to it that you're sorry.' But that could only mean he was threatenin' him. Hightower already told him he'd have his license, so what else was left?"

Mrs. Jeffries sighed. Really, people were so good at hearing what they wanted to hear. "Did you tell Inspector Witherspoon about this?"

"No. I didn't want him thinking I was the kind to sneak around behind my employer's back," she replied defensively. "It'd make me look awful bad. Make me look like if I'd sneak back here one time, I'd do it again. Do you know what I mean?"

"Yes, I think I do, but you've got to tell him what you overheard as soon as possible. There's no time to lose. Will you do it?"

Effie chewed nervously on her lower lip as she thought about it. "If you think I should."

"Good." Mrs. Jeffries rose to her feet. Her mind was frantically trying to put together all these new pieces of the puzzle. Luty Belle Crookshank was convinced that Dr. Slocum hadn't died of mushroom poisoning. Mrs. Beals claimed that Catherine Leslie had once been a patient of Slocum's and that Hightower had threatened the man. Keating was frightened of people telling tales, and on top of everything, the victim was going to change his will. And then there was the matter of the calling cards and the key.

"Mrs. Beals, did Dr. Slocum have a key?"

"He had lots of keys. But Keating would know more about that than I would. He's the butler. Hangin' on to keys is his job."

"Yes, but did he have one particular key that he kept on his person? One that he didn't give to the butler?"

Effie's brows drew together in concentration. Suddenly, she smiled. "Oh yes, that's right. He did have a key, a little gold one he wore on his watch chain. But I never seen him use it."

"Meaning you don't know what the key unlocked?" Mrs. Jeffries stared at her in disappointment as the cook shook her head. "Oh dear, that's a shame. I suspect that key may be important."

"Sorry, but like I said, I never seen him use it. Tell you what. Why don't I have a snoop around and see if I can find out what it went to? It were just a small key, so maybe whatever it opened is still around here somewhere."

"That's a good idea," Mrs. Jeffries said. "Let me know if you're successful. I've got to be going now, but if you think of anything else that may be helpful, send a footman around with a note and I'll come right away."

She gave the cook her address and then turned toward the hall, intending to leave the way she'd come.

She stopped near the door and gazed around the large kitchen. "Are you sure that the back door was locked on the day that Dr. Slocum was murdered?"

"Positive. I locked it myself."

"But someone got into this house that day? How?"

"Could have come in through the window." Effie pointed to the sink. Above it was a large open window. "That was unlocked. I told the police that, but they didn't think it was important. But I reckon that's how the murderer got in."

"Why was the window open? I thought Dr. Slocum was terribly concerned about burglars?"

"He was, but I'd cooked fish the night before and the smell was awful, so Keating told me to leave the window open and he'd make sure it was shut before he left. But he didn't. It was still open when I got back from Chelmsford that evening."

Mrs. Jeffries added this new piece of information to everything else she'd found out this morning. "Keating told you to keep it open?" she repeated. "Are you certain of that?"

"Absolutely. It's not the sort of thing I'm likely to be mistaken about."

Mrs. Jeffries had arranged to meet Betsy on Brompton Road, where they would board an omnibus together and return to Upper Edmonton Gardens.

Betsy was fairly dancing with excitement when she spotted Mrs. Jeffries walking briskly up the road. She picked up her long skirts and raced toward her.

"Oh, Mrs. Jeffries," she gasped. "I've found out ever so much. You'll be ever so pleased."

"I'm sure I will," the housekeeper said calmly. "But let's wait until we're on board the omnibus before you begin."

She took the girl's arm, and they dodged between hansoms, carriages and various other traffic to cross the busy thoroughfare.

The omnibus pulled up just as they reached the other side. They climbed aboard and went up top, where they found two seats in relative privacy near the back.

"Now, tell me what you've found out," Mrs. Jeffries demanded softly.

Betsy giggled. "This detectin's hard work, I can tell you that. I must have walked two miles this morning gettin' that boy from Colonel Seaward's to chat."

"You made the acquaintance of someone from the Seaward household?" Mrs. Jeffries exclaimed.

"Yes, but that's not important. What is, is that I run into Rosie Scrimmons—we knows each other from back when I used to live over Whitechapel way. But she was with this woman called Maisie Logan, and Maisie's a special friend of that butler, Keating. Inn't that a bit of luck?"

"Yes, it certainly is," Mrs. Jeffries replied. "Go on, Betsy. What did this Miss Logan tell you?"

"Well, this 'ere Keating, he drinks like a fish."

"I suspected that might be the case."

"And not only that, he's been flashin' a lot o' money about." Betsy broke off and blushed. "Maisie's not exactly respectable, but she's a right talker. When I said she was Keating's 'special friend,' I meant that he's keepin' her."

Mrs. Jeffries stared incredulously at the maid. "Precisely what do you mean by that?" She saw Betsy's blush turn a bright crimson. "Oh dear, are you implying she's a . . ."

"Lady of the evening," Betsy finished lamely. "Look 'ere, I know I shouldn't be consortin' with the likes o' Maisie Logan, but she's not a bad sort, and she don't have any other way to make a livin'. Besides, I knows how to talk to 'er. It's not all that long ago that I was livin' in the slums meself."

"It's all right, Betsy," Mrs. Jeffries assured her, reaching over to pat her hand. "I wasn't passing judgment. I'm merely surprised that a person in that particular profession would be up so early. Now what did Maisie tell you?"

"She told me that Keating was one of 'er regulars like, but that about six months ago, he began wanting 'er all to hisself. Didn't want her walkin' the streets no more. Well, Maisie soon told 'im that was no good. A girl's got to make a livin', so Keating started takin' care of her. Payin' her rent and buyin' her things. She says she thinks he suddenly come into a bit o' money, and that he's always boastin' he's got lots more squirreled away." She broke off and snorted. "Mind you, Rosie told me that Maisie still works a bit on the side."

"Goodness, Betsy," Mrs. Jeffries said earnestly. "You've done very well. Fancy getting so much information in such a short time."

Betsy giggled. "Well, like I said, I knows how to get 'em to start talkin'."

"Did you get any information about the key?"

She shook her head. "No, nobody knew anythin' about a key. I'm afraid I didn't get any new information about any of the others either."

"Nothing at all?"

"Just what we've already heard. That Dr. Hightower was carryin' on with Mrs. Leslie and the whole neighborhood knew about it."

Mrs. Jeffries frowned. If it was common knowledge that Catherine Leslie and Dr. Hightower were carrying on an illicit relationship, there wouldn't be any point in Slocum trying to blackmail them. Therefore, neither of them would have a motive to murder him.

"Frankly, I'm not certain how to interpret any of this. We've obtained an enormous amount of information this morning. I've learned quite a bit myself." She quickly filled Betsy in on her meeting with Mrs. Crookshank and her conversation with Effie Beals.

"I don't suppose you learned anything more about Colonel Seaward?" Mrs. Jeffries asked as she ended her narrative.

"Nothing important," Betsy admitted. "The footman I talked to said the same thing as the inspector. Colonel Seaward was with his guests from eleven until two."

"The whole time?" Mrs. Jeffries asked the question halfheartedly. Seaward was the only person on the gardens who didn't have a reason for wanting to murder Dr. Slocum.

Betsy shrugged. "More or less. David did say he left the room for a bit whilst he nipped down to the cellar to get a special bottle of wine. But he weren't gone for more than a few minutes. He said that Seaward's a right good employer, treats the servants properly and all." She shook her head. "It's as plain as the spots on Wiggins's face that the colonel couldn't have done it. And if'n what that Mrs. Crookshank says is true, maybe no one done it! Could be Slocum wasn't even murdered."

"I doubt that's true," Mrs. Jeffries said softly. "We may find out he wasn't poisoned by a mushroom, but I think we can safely assume he didn't die of natural causes."

"What makes you think so?" Betsy stared at her quizzically.

"Because of Dr. Hightower. He wouldn't have sent for the police if he thought Dr. Slocum's death wasn't suspicious."

Mrs. Jeffries lapsed into concentration, trusting that Betsy would nudge her when they reached their destination.

The trouble with this affair, she thought, was there were too many loose ends. Catherine Leslie, Effie Beals, Keating, Colonel Seaward and Dr. Hightower. Even Luty Belle Crookshank—they were all connected in some way with the victim. But was one of them his murderer?

Mrs. Jeffries sighed sadly, hoping that the hangman's noose wasn't tightening around Effie Beals's thick neck.

Mrs. Jeffries brightened somewhat when they returned home. Smythe was back. She found him in the kitchen being fussed over by Mrs. Goodge.

He looked up from a plate of currant buns and gave her a cocky grin. "Hello, Mrs. J. I bet you're wondering where I've been the past couple o' days."

"How very astute of you, Smythe," she replied, taking the seat across from him and pouring herself a cup of tea from the pot on the table. "Your whereabouts have crossed my mind a time or two, but knowing how resourceful and clever you are, I realized you probably had a good reason for staying away so long."

He threw back his head and laughed. Mrs. Goodge walked up behind him and nudged him in the shoulder. "Get on with you, Smythe," she said testily. "We all know you've been snooping round on the murder, so stop keepin' us on the edge of our chairs and tell us what you've been up to."

"Give a body time to have some tea," he protested. "I only got here two minutes ago."

"You've got your tea," Betsy interjected, taking the seat next to the housekeeper. "And we're all dyin' of curiosity, so don't be playin' with us like a cat tormentin' a mouse. We know you've been up to somethin'.''

He ignored Betsy and turned his attention to Mrs. Jeffries. "The last time we was all here, you told me to go out and find someone from the Slocum household. Well, I struck gold and ran into that butler, Keating."

"Very good, Smythe," Mrs. Jeffries murmured.

"He's quite a talker when 'e's in 'is cups too," the coachman continued. "And it don't take much to get 'im there neither."

"So what did you learn?" Betsy interrupted impatiently. "We 'aven't got all day, you know. The inspector's going to be here soon."

Smythe shot her a quick frown but continued. "Like I was tryin' to say before I was so rudely interrupted, Keating's a right talker. He was rantin' and ravin' about what a miserable old man Dr. Slocum was. I'd just got him to jabberin' about the murder, when all of a sudden, he glances up and then he snaps his mouth shut. So I looks too. There was a gentleman standin' by the door, a-noddin' to Keating."

He paused and took a sip of tea. "Then Keating hightails it out like a fox runnin' from the hounds. I knew you'd want me to keep an eye on 'im, so I give 'im a minute or two and follows 'im out. You'll never guess what I saw, neither."

Betsy rolled her eyes. Mrs. Goodge snorted, and even Mrs. Jeffries sighed impatiently. "I'm sure we won't, Smythe, so why don't you tell us?"

"Well, I crept up as close as I could and then ducked into a doorway. Keating was standing in the middle of the mews with this 'ere man. They talked for a minute or two, then I saw Keating slip something from his pocket and give it to the other bloke."

"Could you see what it was?" Betsy asked.

"No. It was wrapped in paper. Then they left, but they each went in a different direction and I wasn't sure who to follow, but I reckoned I knew where the butler lived so decided to follow the other un."

Mrs. Jeffries nodded approvingly. "Excellent."

Warmed by the praise, Smythe's chest expanded another inch or two. "Glad I did too, 'cause it worked out right nice. You'll not believe this, but he goes to Howard's livery and rents a carriage. I waited till he was on his way, then I hitched up the horses to the inspector's carriage and took off after 'im. Bow and Arrow is good horses too, caught up with him straightaway, but I stayed far enough back so that he didn't know he was bein' followed."

"You took the carriage out after dark." Mrs. Goodge was outraged. "How foolish. You could have been killed, man. That's not at all safe."

"Don't fret, Mrs. Goodge," Smythe said kindly, used to her fussing. "There was a full moon that night and I lit the lamps. Besides, I've done it before. Miss Euphemia used to love going out in the carriage at night—"

"Yes, yes, we know." Mrs. Jeffries said impatiently. She didn't want Smythe sidetracked by tales about Inspector Witherspoon's rather eccentric late aunt. "Please get on with it. What happened after you left London?"

"Not much until we got to Essex. A few miles outside of Colchester, he pulls into a lane and stops at a cottage. I couldn't follow him any further so I went on past, found a layby to pull off the road and nipped back. I waited long enough to see him light the lamps and figured he must live there, so I knew he wasn't goin' nowhere. I couldn't leave the carriage in the road, so I went on into Colchester and stabled the horses. Then I slipped back and waited." He grinned again. "This is the good part. The next morning, he goes into Colchester and stops at one of them fancy shops."

"What kind of fancy shop?" Mrs. Jeffries asked.

"The kind that sells rich peoples' whatnots. Silly stuff like—broaches and music boxes, china birds and silver bits and pieces. You know what I mean." He waved his hands for emphasis. "I managed to hang about outside, and I watched him through the window. He pulls whatever Keating had given him out of his pocket, takes the paper off and hands it to the shopkeeper. A few minutes later, he's gettin' a fistful of pound notes in return."

"Were you able to see what it was?" Betsy asked.

Smythe shrugged. "I couldn't really see from that distance, but it was small and it was silver."

"Pity you didn't have a chance to go inside and find out," Mrs. Jeffries murmured.

"Couldn't. He came back out, and I didn't want to let him out of my sight."

The sound of footsteps on the pavement outside the kitchen window had Mrs. Jeffries leaping to her feet. "Oh dear, that's the inspector. He's home early."

"How can you tell that's him?" Betsy asked. She was always looking for ways to improve her detecting skills.

Mrs. Jeffries was already heading for the stairs. "His footsteps," she called over her shoulder. "They're quite distinctive."

"Footsteps," murmured Betsy with a puzzled frown.

Mrs. Jeffries opened the front door with a welcoming smile just as Inspector Witherspoon was fishing for his keys. "Good afternoon, sir. How delightful. You've come home early for a change."

"Good afternoon, Mrs. Jeffries," he answered, stepping inside and automatically shedding his coat and hat. "I was close by and decided to come home. It's been quite a day. I haven't even had lunch."

"Then we'll have Mrs. Goodge fix you a nice, substantial tea." Mrs. Jeffries nodded to Betsy, who'd followed her up the stairs.

As soon as the maid hurried in the direction of the kitchen, she turned to the inspector and said, "Why don't you come into the drawing room and have a rest? Betsy will bring the tea when it's ready."

She was eager to hear what he'd learned today.

"I knew you'd be dying of curiosity, Mrs. Jeffries," he said as he settled into his favorite chair. "So as you requested yesterday, I'm going to give you a full accounting."

"Inspector, how kind of you. Please begin. I'm all ears." She took her chair across from him and smiled encouragingly.

Witherspoon gave her a weak half-grin in return and quickly lowered his gaze. She noticed how apprehensive the poor man was. He sat as rigid as a post, his fingers nervously fiddling with his watch chain. But it would do no good to rush him. She could guess what was wrong with the dear man, but he'd tell her about it in his own good time.

"It was just as I thought," he began. "Keating has confirmed my suspicion. Slocum did give the servants the afternoon off directly following his going out and passing out his calling cards. Mind you, finding that out took a bit of doing. I had to question the butler and the other servants for half and hour before we were able to discover that one simple fact."

"Gracious," said Mrs. Jeffries. "That must cast considerable doubt on Mrs. Beal's guilt."

"I'm not sure," he replied glumly. "Nothing in this case is what it seems to be. As to the cook's guilt or innocence, I'm still looking into that. Naturally, though, the more complex the situation becomes, the deeper I dig."

"And what has your digging uncovered?" She gave him another encouraging smile.

"Quite a bit, actually. Today I sent Constable Barnes around to every house in the square. I wanted to know who the doctor had called upon the morning of the murder." He frowned slightly. "It's really quite peculiar. He only left calling cards at Colonel Seaward's and Mrs. Leslie's, but, of course, he left Dr. Hightower's there as well, so I suppose that counts as three."

Mrs. Jeffries didn't find it in the least peculiar. She already knew it. "Really? Isn't that rather outrageous, leaving a calling card at a woman's house for a man who isn't her husband? What a revolting thing to do. By the way, how long has Mrs. Leslie been widowed?"

Three years. Her husband was a wealthy manufacturer in
Birmingham. When he died, Mrs. Leslie sold his factory and
moved to London." Witherspoon shook his head. "Rather
sad, really. The late Mr. Leslie was only in his forties when
he popped off with a rather sudden stomach ailment."

"Yes, one never knows when the good Lord will call one
home, does one?" She wondered if she should start hinting
that Slocum was a blackmailer. But she decided against it.
She wanted to hear the rest of Smythe's story before she
steered the inspector in a new direction. Who knew what
she'd learn next? So far there was blackmail and theft.

"No, one doesn't." Witherspoon sighed. "Bit strange,
though. I wonder why Colonel Seaward didn't mention the
calling card when I was questioning him. Oh well, perhaps
the gentleman merely forgot."

"Yes, I expect you're right," Mrs. Jeffries murmured.
There were moments when she really had to bite her tongue.
Colonel Seaward hadn't forgotten; he just hadn't wanted to
admit any closer acquaintance with the murder victim than
necessary. But then again, she thought, Mrs. Leslie and Dr.
Hightower hadn't admitted that Slocum had dropped his
cards there either. The inspector would never have found
out if the gardener hadn't told him.

"I'm afraid my day got progressively worse after talking
with Keating," Witherspoon admitted morosely.

"I'm sorry to hear that," Mrs. Jeffries said sympathetically. "What happened?"

"Oh, you'll never believe it. After I'd gone back to the
Yard, who should pop in but that Mrs. Crookshank. You
remember, I told you about her. She's that rather forceful
American woman who lives in the house next door to
Slocum's."

"Really? And what did she want?"

His eyes narrowed as he leaned forward. "I don't know
what to make of what she said. She had some sort of out-
landish notion that Dr. Slocum hadn't died of mushroom
poisoning."

"No!" Mrs. Jeffries surreptitiously crossed her fingers.

"Yes," the inspector exclaimed. "And on top of that, she made this accusation just as the chief inspector happened to come in. Of course he asked her to explain herself. She claimed she'd seen several cases of mushroom poisoning in her native country and that Dr. Slocum didn't die from it." Witherspoon looked thoroughly confused now. "So you can see, it's very difficult now. The whole matter's got horribly muddled. Mrs. Crookshank freely admits that 'death caps,' or 'dead eyes' as she persists in calling them, are very lethal. But she also insists it takes several days before one actually dies."

"Gracious!" Could it possibly be true? Do you think she knows what she's talking about?"

"Unfortunately, what I think doesn't matter. The chief inspector called the police surgeon in and started questioning him." He snorted. "And that Mrs. Crookshank wasn't shy about putting her oar in either. She had the gall to ask Dr. Bainbridge, that's Sir Reginald's son, by the way, exactly how many cases of mushroom poisoning he'd treated. Well, it was most embarrassing."

"How many had he treated?"

"To be precise, none. But that doesn't give Mrs. Crookshank the right to laugh in Dr. Bainbridge's face. Nor does it mean that he was mistaken," Witherspoon explained defensively. Suddenly, he broke off and stared glumly into space for a moment before adding, "But I rather think he was mistaken. Even worse, so does the chief inspector. The poor man practically admitted he barely touched the body. He based his entire diagnosis on finding that mushroom piece at the bottom of the soup bowl. Well, one can understand that. You've got a corpse and you've got a bowl with a poisoned mushroom in it—the conclusion is obvious."

"What is going to happen now? Will the investigation continue?"

"Most definitely. Dr. Bainbridge is still certain the deceased was poisoned. We should know more tomorrow—

they're doing another postmortem tonight." Witherspoon grimaced. "Won't be a very nice task, I should think. After all, Slocum's been dead now a good few days."

"Won't you have to . . ." She wrinkled her nose. "Exhume the body?"

"No, actually we've got lucky on that. Slocum's remains were sent to the mortuary, but they haven't been buried yet. His solictor is still ill and hasn't had time to make the funeral arrangements. Lucky for us the man had the gout. Otherwise, we'd have had to dig the old boy up."

Betsy brought in the tea tray. "Tea is ready," she announced. She caught Mrs. Jeffries's eyes and jerked her chin meaningfully toward the kitchen.

Mrs. Jeffries waited until the inspector had tucked into a plate of sandwiches, excused herself and then dashed back to the kitchen.

Everyone was sitting at the table. Smythe had obviously not said another word, because Betsy and Mrs. Goodge were glaring at him and Wiggins was watching them all warily.

"Smythe, go ahead and finish your report," she commanded softly as she took a chair.

"What report?" Wiggins asked.

"Later, Wiggins," Betsy promised. "Right now we want him to finish up."

"There's not much more to tell," Smythe replied. "I spent the rest of the time keepin' my eye on him, but he didn't do much. It wasn't until last night that he went out again and that was to a pub."

"So you've spent the past few days skulkin' round Colchester and that's all you've found out," Betsy said accusingly.

"What was 'e doin' in Colchester?" Wiggins asked. Everyone ignored him.

"I didn't say that, now, did I? If you must know, I've found out quite a bit about this gentleman," Smythe answered testily. "And I wasn't skulking about. I was standing in the cold and wind and doing my duty so our inspector won't end up with egg on his face."

"Now, now, no one's accusing you of dereliction of duty, Smythe," Mrs. Jeffries interjected hastily. "And we are very curious about what you've learned."

That soothed his ruffled feather's some. "Well, like I was saying before I was interrupted." He glared at Betsy. "I waited until after the toff left, then I started asking questions about him. It seems he's been living above his means for the past few years and owed everyone in town. But recently, he's come into a bit and is payin' off his creditors. It's my opinion he's payin' 'em off by sellin' the stuff Keating's been slipping him."

"That's a reasonable assumption," Mrs. Jeffries said calmly. "Go on."

"And the man can't hold his liquor neither. Spends most nights drinking in his local pub. But lately, he hasn't been around much." Smythe paused and then said dramatically, "He wasn't at his local or his home the day that Dr. Slocum was murdered, neither. He was in London."

"Very good, Smythe." Mrs. Jeffries beamed like a schoolteacher at an especially gifted student. "And now why don't you give us the most important news of all."

"I thought I was doing just that," he protested, but he was breaking into another one of his cocky grins. "All right, Mrs. J, I reckon I should have known better than to try and keep you guessing."

"What's he talking about?" Mrs. Goodge scowled at the both of them.

"I'm talking about the name of the man I've been watchin' for the past few days. The man I followed this morning to a squalid little 'otel off the Brompton Road. It's the dead man's nephew. Joshua Slocum."

CHAPTER 9

"You could have told us that before," Betsy protested.

"Does that mean the old man's nephew murdered him?" Wiggins asked. He glanced around the table in confusion.

"Humph," Mrs. Goodge snorted. "You just like to play about, don't you, Smythe? Well, I tell you this 'ere is murder we're talking about—"

"Now, now," Mrs. Jeffries said soothingly. "Let's all keep calm. I'm sure Smythe wasn't deliberately withholding the name of the gentleman for purely dramatic effect. He's far too sensible for nonsense like that." She looked at the coachman.

"Certainly not," he said innocently, trying to keep from breaking out in a grin. "But that's not important now. What is important is that I figures Joshua Slocum only comes into London when he's wanting to meet that crooked butler and pick up a few more goodies. This is our chance, Mrs. Jeffries. I reckons there's a bit o' theft to be going on tonight."

"Get on with you, Smythe," Betsy burst out. "Why should Joshua Slocum keep stealing from the house? He's the heir. He owns everything now."

"The heir! How do you know that?" he shot back irritably.

"Mrs. Jeffries told us," Betsy said smugly. "While you was off diddling about in the country, we wasn't sittin' 'ere twiddling our thumbs. You're not the only one who can find things out."

His face fell and he looked at Mrs. Jeffries. "Is it true?"

"Yes it is," she admitted. "Joshua Slocum is Bartholomew Slocum's heir. But we don't know that he knew that very important fact. Remember, Keating had told Mrs. Beals that the doctor was changing his will. No doubt, he told Joshua as well."

"How'd ya find out all that?" Smythe asked.

Mrs. Jeffries quickly filled the coachman in on all the information they'd learned to date. She finished her narrative by telling everyone about Witherspoon's unfortunate encounter with Mrs. Crookshank and the second post-mortem.

"So you see," she concluded, "many of our previous assumptions about the manner of Dr. Slocum's death may now have been proven false. Therefore, we can't afford to overlook anything. Joshua Slocum may have had every reason to keep right on stealing from the house—as far as he knows, he's already been disinherited. There's no evidence that Keating or any of the household knew the new will had been delayed."

"And even if he did know, he was the heir," Betsy pointed out. "He still won't get a penny till this 'ere murder is solved. If'n what Smythe says is true and he was in London on the day of the murder, he's bound to be a suspect and I knows you can't profit from a crime. Inn't that right, Mrs. Jeffries?"

"That's absolutely correct." She smiled proudly at Betsy. "How on earth did you know that?"

"From them 'orrible Kensington High Street murders. I overheard you and the inspector discussin' it."

"Hmm. Very good, Betsy." She glanced at the clock on the mantel. "However, back to our immediate problem. I suspect that Smythe in absolutely correct. There is going to be another theft tonight. Hurry, Smythe. You and Wiggins dash upstairs and put some warm clothes on."

"Warm clothes?" Wiggins complained. "What do we need warm clothes for?"

Smythe was already getting to his feet. "Whaddaya think, you knot-head?" he snapped. He was still a bit put out over Betsy's superior knowledge of British law. " 'Cause tonight we're goin' to catch a thief."

Tendrils of fog floated through the darkness of the mews behind the pub. Betsy huddled closer to Mrs. Jeffries and pulled her cloak tighter. " 'Ow much longer? My feet are gettin' cold."

"You didn't have to come," Smythe shot back before the housekeeper could reply. "You and Mrs. Jeffries should 'ave stayed 'ome with Mrs. Goodge. This 'ere is men's work—"

"Ha, you and Wiggins? Don't be daft."

"What do you mean by that?" Wiggins hissed indignantly.

"Hush, all of you," Mrs. Jeffries interjected. "If you don't keep still, someone's going to get the constable."

They were standing behind the pub, waiting for Joshua Slocum to show up. Keating was already inside. They'd followed him from the Slocum house and that hadn't been easy, considering there were four of them. Betsy, when she'd realized that Mrs. Jeffries meant to go, wouldn't hear of being left behind herself.

Suddenly the door of the pub opened. In the brief light, Mrs. Jeffries recognized the butler. He stepped into the mews and turned his head.

Smythe, Wiggins, Betsy and Mrs. Jeffries all crowded closer in the passageway where they were hiding. A few moments later, they heard the sound of boot steps approaching from the opposite end of the mews.

Smythe leaned his head out of the passageway. "It's him."

"I've got ta sneeze," Wiggins moaned.

"Nell's bells." The coachman shot the boy a disgusted

look. "This is the last time I take you anywhere."

Wiggins grasped his chin and made a squeaky, keening noise.

"Hold your nose," Mrs. Jeffries advised softly. "We can't risk being seen."

From the mews, they heard the murmur of voices, and she raised her hand for silence. They cocked their heads toward the sound, except for Wiggins, who was holding onto his nose and lolling his head from side to side.

"What's he doing?" Betsy whispered. "I can't see. Wiggins's fat ol' 'ead's in me way."

"'E's not doing nuthin','" Smythe answered, crouching low and peering out the passage. "They's just standin' there. Talking. You want me to grab 'em?"

His last statement was directed at Mrs. Jeffries.

She shook her head negatively.

A moment later, both men started walking in the direction of Brompton Road.

Smythe stood up and started to follow. Mrs. Jeffries laid a restraining hand on his arm. "Not yet," she murmured. "Let's give them time to get to the end of the mews."

Wiggins lost the battle. He sneezed loudly. "Sorry," he muttered defensively, as three heads turned and three pairs of eyes glared at him accusingly.

A moment later, Mrs. Jeffries judged that the men had had time to reach the road. She jerked her head, and they started off.

The quartet followed the two men through Knightsbridge, dodging back and forth across the quiet streets to avoid gas lamps and patrolling constables.

When they arrived at their destination, Mrs. Jeffries wasn't surprised to see the two men disappear inside Dr. Slocum's house.

"What'll we do now?" Smythe asked.

"It's quite simple," she replied, heading up the stairs. "We go inside."

Smythe grabbed her elbow. "Look, Mrs. J. I think I'd better 'andle this." He leapt ahead of her, raced up the stairs and banged the knocker before she could protest.

Keating opened the door. "What do you want, knocking this time of the night?" he demanded. "If you've come to see the doctor, you're too late, he's dead."

"Oh, we've come about the doctor, all right," Smythe replied hotly, not liking being addressed so rudely. "And if you knows what's good for ya, ya'd best be lettin' us in before I goes to call the constable. He'd like to hear about that nice bit o' thievin' you and Mr. Slocum's got for yourselves."

The butler's jaw dropped. Mrs. Jeffries quickly stepped in front of the coachman. "Keating, it's me, Hepzibah Jeffries, Inspector Witherspoon's housekeeper. Please let us in. We must talk to you and to Mr. Slocum."

"What's going on?" The thin, pale face of Joshua Slocum appeared behind the butler. "Who are these people? What do they want?"

Keating didn't answer. He was still gaping at the burly, threatening Smythe.

"May we please come in?" Mrs. Jeffries said in her most imperious tone. She wasn't overly concerned about their safety. Mrs. Goodge had been left with strict instructions that if they weren't back by midnight, she was to awaken the inspector and tell him everything. And she also knew that despite her objections, Smythe had stuck a rather wicked-looking hunting knife in his boot. She had a feeling he knew how to use it too.

Joshua Slocum scowled at them. "Who the devil are you?"

"It's that police inspector's housekeeper." Keating moaned. He started wringing his hands together.

"I fail to see how that's of any consequence," the young man blustered, but he stared at them uncertainly.

"I'm afraid our presence here is very consequential, sir," Mrs. Jeffries said. "Unless you'd rather speak with Inspector

Witherspoon himself about the murder of your late uncle, I suggest you let us inside."

Without waiting for permission, Keating pulled the door open wide. "We'd better do as she says. They knows about us."

Slocum glared at them sullenly as they filed past and followed the butler into the drawing room. Mrs. Jeffries watched Slocum as they settled themselves into chairs.

He continued to stand. His mouth was compressed into a thin, flat line, his pale face had gone a ghastly white, and beneath the bluster and arrogance in his eyes, she could see he was afraid. He lifted his chin and met her gaze.

She heard him take a deep breath.

"Now what the devil do you people want?" he said.

"Mr. Slocum," Mrs. Jeffries replied. "We want the truth. A woman's life may depend on it."

"If you're talking about the old boy's murder, I don't know anything about that—"

She raised her hand for silence. "We know all about your and Keating's thefts."

"You can't prove anything," Slocum blustered, "and furthermore, a man can't be arrested for selling his own property."

"Yes, but it wasn't your property until very recently was it? These thefts have been going on for a long time, haven't they? At least six months."

Slocum stared at her in amazement for a moment and then slumped against the wall. "Just tell us what you want and get out of here."

"Watch your manners, boy," Smythe snarled.

"I want you to answer some questions," Mrs. Jeffries stated firmly. "And please, don't try to lie to us. We know you were in London on the day your uncle was murdered. But what I want to know now is where were you exactly?"

Keating moaned.

Slocum shot him a quick, open glance of disgust. "I was

at my hotel all day." He sneered.

"Really? That's not what the porter says," Mrs. Jeffries replied. She ignored the fact that Betsy, Smythe and Wiggins were staring at her curiously. She only hoped that Joshua Slocum hadn't noticed. She had no more spoken to the porter than she'd had tea with the Queen.

"According to the porter, you left your room quite early that morning and didn't return until late that afternoon." She tilted her chin to one side and gazed at him speculatively. "Come now, why don't you save yourself a lot of pain and grief? Tell us the truth. Where were you?"

"For God's sakes, tell her," Keating shouted. "Can't you see, she already knows."

"Shut up, you fool," Slocum blazed.

"You were here that day, weren't you?" Mrs. Jeffries asked calmly. She silently breathed a sigh of relief that her gamble had worked.

All the bluster left Slocum then. He stared at her for a long moment, then sighed and buried his face in his hands. "Yes. I was here," he muttered softly.

"Did you see your uncle?" Betsy interjected.

Slocum laughed bitterly. "No, that was the last thing I wanted to do. I was hiding in the attic."

Mrs. Jeffries gazed at him thoughtfully. "Did you poison Bartholomew Slocum?"

He lifted his head and shook it slowly. "No, I hated the old man, but I didn't kill him."

"Then why were you hiding in the attic?"

"Because that's where Uncle Bartholomew kept the things he'd lost interest in. I was looking for something to steal." He sighed. "But I don't rightly think of it as stealing. More like reclaiming my own property."

Smythe snorted.

"It's true," Slocum protested. He gestured around the room with his hand. "All of this, by rights, should belong to me. If that miserable old blackguard hadn't blackmailed our Uncle Thaddeus, it would be mine."

"Dr. Slocum blackmailed your uncle?" Mrs. Jeffries asked.

"Yes. That's how he got started in his evil ways, not that he was ever a particularly good man."

"When did this happen?"

"It was eleven years ago. I remember because it was the year I left school," Slocum explained. "Uncle Bartholomew had come out to Colchester to try and make up with our Uncle Thaddeus. Uncle Thaddeus was my guardian, and I lived with him, of course. But Thaddeus stupidly broke his leg. While he was in Bartholomew's care, he admitted he'd embezzled his partners in a business venture."

"You mean he just came out and confessed bein' an embezzler to a nephew he didn't even like?" Smythe asked with disbelief in his voice.

"No, no, that wasn't Bartholomew's way. He used some sort of medicine to get Thaddeus to talk. Some awful kind of potion that kills the pain. I don't know what it was called." He looked up defensively. "But I do know that if you pump someone full of this stuff and then start asking questions, he'll talk his fool head off."

"Hmm," murmured Mrs. Jeffries. "I wonder if he was using opium on his patients."

"I don't know." Slocum shrugged and looked down at the floor. "But whatever kind of brew he used, it worked. At least on Uncle Thaddeus, and before you could say Bob's your uncle, Bartholomew was the new heir and I was left out in the cold. Then Thaddeus up and died the next year, and I've been living hand-to-mouth ever since."

"So that was probably Dr. Slocum's first successful attempt at blackmail," Mrs. Jeffries said. She watched to see if Slocum would react. But he didn't, and she knew then that he was fully aware of how his late uncle's nefarious activities began.

Slocum shrugged. "What does it matter, first or not. It worked and he ended up with my fortune."

"So you decided to steal it back from 'im?" Betsy said.

The butler moaned again, but everyone ignored him. They were all staring at Joshua.

He cleared his throat. "Yes, I did decide to steal it back from him. Why shouldn't I? It should have been mine. But that doesn't make me a murderer."

"Why should we believe you?" Mrs. Jeffries said softly.

"Why should I want him dead?"

"You were his heir."

"But I didn't know that till a couple of days ago." Slocum grinned triumphantly. "I thought dear Uncle Bartholomew had changed his will. I didn't know the will had been delayed until Keating told me the other night when I met him behind the pub."

"That was the night I followed 'im to Colchester," Smythe said.

"You followed me?" Slocum stared at him curiously. "Really? I had no idea."

"Course not. I'm bleedin' good at it."

"Gentlemen, please," Mrs. Jeffries interjected sharply. "We don't have time to digress. Mr. Slocum, will you please continue."

"Like I said, I was in the house to find something else to take," he admitted honestly. "But I didn't kill him. Keating and I were going through the attic. No one ever goes up there." He smiled slyly. "And the place is crammed full of expensive trinkets that Bartholomew had lost interest in."

Mrs. Jeffries frowned slightly. "Why did you pick that particular day?"

"I always came on a Wednesday. Bartholomew's surgery was closed and half the servants were gone. It was perfect. If by chance my dear uncle stayed home, whoever was in the house generally had to wait on him hand and foot."

"But that day, your uncle gave everyone the day off," Smythe said. "That must have put a spoke in your wheels."

"It did."

Mrs. Jeffries leaned forward eagerly. Betsy straightened her spine, and Wiggins almost fell off the edge of his seat in his eagerness to hear the rest. Smythe reached out a hand and pulled him back as he slid toward the floor.

"I'd been up there less than ten minutes when Keating came dashing in and told me all the servants were being given the day off," Slocum continued. "We knew our plan was ruined then, because that meant Keating had to leave too and I didn't want to actually leave the house with anything on my person. It was too risky if Bartholomew happened to catch me."

Puzzled, Betsy asked, "If you didn't carry the goods away, why did you risk coming here in the first place?"

"Because I knew what would fetch the most money. Keating couldn't tell a piece of Dresden from a cheap china cat."

Keating's mouth flattened to a thin line, but he kept silent.

"Did you see or hear anything as you were leaving the house?" Mrs. Jeffries asked impatiently. Really, she thought, if he didn't hurry up, they'd be here all night.

He nodded. "I was halfway down the stairs, just outside of Bartholomew's bedroom, when some of the servants came up to get their coats. I ducked into the bedroom, thinking I'd wait till everyone left and then get out by the servants' steps."

"What time was this?" Betsy asked.

"About five minutes to twelve or thereabouts. That's a guess, as I didn't bother to check my watch. So I waited for a few minutes, and then I peeked over the stairs and saw the cook walking down the hall with Bartholomew's lunch tray. Well, I thought it would be prudent to wait a few more minutes before leaving—I didn't want to run into any last-minute stragglers in the kitchen. But just as I decided to risk it, I heard another set of footsteps."

"And who was that?" Smythe asked, not wanting to be outshone by Betsy.

"I don't know, but it wasn't any of the servants."

"How can you be sure of that?" Mrs. Jeffries asked.

"Because whoever it was went into the surgery, and the servants would never do that. Bartholomew had strict rules about the surgery. Even the maid wasn't allowed in except for early in the morning when she did the cleaning."

"Could it have been Dr. Slocum?" Mrs. Jeffries asked.

"No, Keating had told me he was in his study, and you can see the study door from the top of the stairs. The door was still closed when I came out of the attic." He shook his head. "I knew he was in there. But as you can imagine, by this time I was beginning to get nervous. Keating had left the house right after he spoke to me, so I was on my own. I waited for a few minutes, and then the footsteps came out of the surgery and down the hall."

"Could you tell if the footsteps went into the dining room?" Surprisingly enough, it was Wiggins who asked this question.

Betsy, Mrs. Jeffries and Smythe all turned and stared at him in amazement.

"No. I couldn't. But Bartholomew was still holed up in his study. Probably scribbling nasty secrets about one of his patients in that ugly little black book of his."

Mrs. Jeffries straightened. "Black book? Do you mean his medical notes?"

"Hardly," Slocum answered with a sneer. "He wasn't that conscientious a doctor. I don't think the man ever recorded a word about what was actually ailing a person. But he did keep records about people's secrets, things they'd tell him in the course of treatment. Or even worse, things he'd get out of them when he was dosing them with one of his evil potions."

"How do you know? Did you ever see this book?" Mrs. Jeffries wasn't sure but that the man was lying. It was a bit too convenient, a written record of other blackmail victims and therefore other murder suspects. She knew it wasn't the need for confession that had loosened Joshua Slocum's tongue tonight. It was fear and shock. No doubt he wanted to throw as much suspicion as possible somewhere else.

"Once. I'd come to ask my beloved uncle for a loan. He was sitting at his desk, scribbling away, a malicious smile on his face as he told me to seek honest employment. That's a laugh, him telling me to find *honest employment*. But he got called downstairs to see a patient, and when he was gone, I took a look at it."

"You mean he just left it sitting on his desk?" Smythe asked cynically.

"Of course not. He locked it in the top drawer. But he was in a hurry and the lock didn't quite catch. It was easy to open the drawer. I took the notebook out and read it."

"What was in the notebook?" Mrs. Jeffries asked cautiously. She wasn't sure she believed any of it.

"Just letters and numbers. I think it might have been a code."

Mrs. Jeffries looked over at the butler. Keating was slumped against the wall, staring morosely at the floor. "Keating."

There was no response. She wondered if he'd been drinking.

"Keating," she repeated loudly.

His head snapped up and he blinked. He stared at her blankly for a moment before his eyes focused. "Yes, ma'am."

"Where is the notebook?"

"Notebook?"

"Yes," she said impatiently, "the notebook. Dr. Slocum's notebook."

"The little black one he usually kept in his study desk," Slocum interjected by way of explanation.

"Oh, that one," Keating said. "I don't know. Don't the police have it? Wasn't it in his desk?"

Mrs. Jeffries started to inform him in no uncertain terms that the police certainly did not have it. Then she clamped her mouth shut, thinking that perhaps the fewer people who knew the notebook wasn't in the possession of Scotland Yard, the better.

But where was it? Witherspoon certainly didn't have it. He would have told her if he'd come across anything as remotely mysterious as a book inscribed in code.

"They may," she lied. She turned to Joshua Slocum. "Did he always keep it locked in his study desk?"

Slocum shrugged. "I have no idea."

"I do," Keating said, pushing away from the door frame and straightening his spine. Gazing at Mrs. Jeffries, he drew himself up to his full height, and for a moment, he grasped an old and possibly forgotten shred of dignity. "Dr. Slocum did not keep the notebook in his desk. It was most valuable to him. He locked it away somewhere known only to himself."

Mrs. Jeffries knew then what the key unlocked. "I suppose," she said to Slocum," that on the day you saw the book, Dr. Slocum wasn't expecting to see you?"

"That's right. He wasn't expecting me. He wasn't expecting anyone. I walked in unannounced and found him working at his desk."

"How very fortuitous for you. You don't, by any chance, happen to have any idea who your uncle was blackmailing, do you?"

Again she watched Slocum carefully, and again he showed no reaction.

"No. But it wouldn't surprise me to find out he had half of London under his control. He was a grasping man. Nothing was ever good enough for Bartholomew. He always wanted more, more, more. More money, more power, more everything." Slocum broke off and laughed bitterly. "You'd have thought a decent practice and one fortune would have been enough for any man. But it wasn't, not for him. I'm glad he's dead. I'm glad someone's finally given that cur what he deserves."

"No doubt," Mrs. Jeffries said briskly as she rose to her feet. Betsy, Smythe and Wiggins got up too. She realized that it was imperative to find that notebook before Joshua Slocum could get his hands on it. She wasn't sure but that he was as capable of blackmail as his late uncle had been. "You've benefited very nicely, haven't you?"

Slocum's face darkened as he flushed. "And why not? It should have been mine by rights anyway."

Mrs. Jeffries turned suddenly to Keating. "Did you leave the house immediately after you'd warned Mr. Slocum?" she asked.

"No, ma'am. Dr. Slocum rang for me just as I was leaving. When I went to the study, he asked me to make sure I'd brought up the right bottle of wine."

"Is there a wrong kind of wine?" Smythe asked sarcastically.

"Yes," Keating replied testily. "Not that I'd expect someone like you to know the difference—"

"From what we 'ear, Slocum wasn't one to know good wine from bad either," Betsy said testily, leaping to Smythe's defense. "The wine merchant was braggin' you could sell 'im any old kind of slog, as long as it 'ad a fancy label on it."

"Unfortunately, that is true." The butler looked embarrassed. "But he did want to make sure I'd brought up a red wine and not a white. He was having lamb for his lunch."

Mrs. Jeffries frowned at Betsy and Smythe before giving Keating a sympathetic smile. "And had you brought a red wine?"

"No. So I had to rush out to the cooling pantry and get one."

"Is the cooling pantry off the kitchen?"

"It's off the kitchen, but you have to go outside and across the terrace to the side of the house. There's no connecting door from inside."

"So you were out on the terrace between . . ." Mrs. Jeffries cocked her head to one side and calculated back. "Quarter to twelve and ten to. Would that be a reasonable assumption?"

Keating nodded.

"Did you see anyone in the gardens?"

"The police have already asked that," he protested. "And

I'll give you the same answer I gave them. I was in a hurry; I didn't want to hang about in case the doctor happened on Joshua somehow, so I didn't have time to look at the ruddy flowers. Even if I had, you can't see very much from that end of the terrace. The only bloomin' thing I saw was a . . ." He faltered and then stopped completely, his face bewildered.

"Keating?" Mrs. Jeffries prompted. "Have you remembered something?"

"Blimey," he exclaimed, "I have. It just now come back to me. When I was rushing across the terrace, I saw something out of the corner of my eye."

Smythe sighed impatiently. "Well, what was it?"

"It was a bit of skirt, a woman's skirt. There was a patch of bright green sticking out from behind the tree across the way."

Betsy's eyes narrowed suspiciously. "Are you trying to tell us someone was hiding behind a tree?"

That was precisely what the butler was trying to tell them. An hour later they were all gathered around the kitchen table back at Upper Edmonton Gardens. Mrs. Goodge was clucking over them like a broody hen and pouring out cups of steaming hot cocoa.

After discussing every aspect of the case thoroughly, they still hadn't decided whether or not the butler was lying. Smythe was sure he was, Betsy was sure he wasn't, and Wiggins couldn't make up his mind.

"How did you know that Slocum had been in the house on the day of the murder?" Smythe finally asked.

Mrs. Jeffries delicately took a sip before answering. "I didn't. That was a lucky guess."

"Cor, blimey," Wiggins exclaimed.

"Who do you think was behind the tree?" asked Betsy. "You know it could 'ave been the cook, Effie Beals."

"No, the one person who wouldn't have had to skulk about in the gardens is Mrs. Beals. Remember, she had a right to be in the house."

"Maybe it was that Mrs. Crookshank," Smythe suggested.

"Perhaps," Mrs. Jeffries said thoughtfully. "Or perhaps it was Catherine Leslie."

"But didn't her maid claim she was lying down that whole morning." Betsy said.

Mrs. Jeffries was pleased that all of them remembered the details of the case so clearly. "The maid could have been lying to protect her mistress, or Mrs. Leslie might have slipped out unbeknownst to the girl."

"I don't know." Smythe shook his head. "I still don't think those two we was talkin' to tonight would know the truth if it walked up and bit 'em in the ars— arm," he amended quickly. "I stills thinks they's lying their 'eads off and there weren't no one hiding behind any tree."

"But why?" Mrs. Jeffries put her cup down and stared at the coachman. He was a very intelligent man, and she had a great deal of respect for his reasoning ability.

"To throw suspicion elsewhere in case one of them gets charged with murder." Smythe jabbed a finger at Betsy. "I was thinkin' on what she said—about not profitin' from a crime. Well, what if Slocum caught 'em that day and they killed him? From what you said, the old boy didn't die from eatin' no mushrooms, but there must have been all kinds of nasty stuff lurkin' about in his surgery. After they'd poisoned his food or even his wine, Keating remembers Mrs. Crookshank goin' on about them mushrooms growin' outside, so he nips out and plants them in the soup bowl and the kitchen so the cook will get the blame."

As a scenario, Mrs. Jeffries had to admit it might be possible. And if Slocum had caught his nephew stealing, she had no doubt that he'd prosecute. "You might be right."

"And I really think you oughts to tell the inspector what we've found out tonight," Smythe continued. "Tellin' Slocum and Keating you're gonna give 'em a chance to go to 'im themselves! If you wants my opinion, and I'm sure you do, that's a bit dicey. We already know they're theives and probably killers too."

"Smythe, you know why I can't tell the inspector anything," Mrs. Jeffries said gently. "He'd be dreadfully hurt if he knew we were assisting him with his cases. He'd think we had no confidence in him. Besides, you will recall that I also told Mr. Slocum and Keating that if they did not voluntarily make a statement to the inspector, I'd see to it myself."

"All right," he replied grudgingly. "But I didn't like 'em and I don't trust them neither."

"Speaking of the inspector," Mrs. Goodge said as she sat another pot of hot chocolate on the table, "he asked me to tell you he'd be leaving especially early for the Yard. So if you want to ask him any questions, you'd best be up early yourself."

Mrs. Jeffries frowned slightly. "Did he say why?"

"He got a message from the Yard this evening. The doctor that did the postmortem, he wants to see him first thing tomorrow morning."

CHAPTER 10

———◦◦◦◦◦———

Mrs. Goodge's announcement caused another stir. Everyone had a different idea about what it meant, so another half hour passed before Mrs. Jeffries escaped to her quarters for a good think.

She sat in the soothing darkness of her room, going over and over every scrap of information she had about the murder of Dr. Bartholomew Slocum. For, indeed, she knew now he had been poisoned, and the lethal dose hadn't been in a mushroom either.

If the original diagnosis of Slocum's death had been correct, the message from the Yard for Inspector Witherspoon would have said exactly that. But it hadn't, and that could mean only one thing. They now knew what had killed the man.

She pulled her wrapper tighter against the chill as she tried to think what the next step should be. For several minutes, she was uncharacteristically unsure of how best to proceed in the investigation. Suddenly, she realized the reason for her uncertainty. She stopped thinking and let her mind wander. Closing her eyes, she took a deep, calming breath. A tendril of an idea nudged at the edge of her mind. She didn't force the thought to come; she let the vague images flow and ebb in their own good time. Before long, the images began to swirl and take shape, forming a nebulous chain of thought.

Her breathing slowed. She was close to the answer. Very close.

Slowly, Mrs. Jeffries opened her eyes as the ideas coalesced into a hard certainty. There was so much to do tomorrow. She had to talk to Catherine Leslie and to Effie Beals. She made a mental note to make sure she took Wiggins and Smythe with her. She'd need them both.

If her suspicions were correct, tomorrow the case would be solved.

Seeing Catherine Leslie was impossible. A petite blond-haired French maid hautily informed Mrs. Jeffries that Mrs. Leslie "wasn't receiving." Upon further questioning, the girl reluctantly admitted she wasn't even at home.

"You will forgive me, madam," the maid said in delicately accented English, "but I fail to see what business you have with my mistress." She cast a rather disparaging glance at Mrs. Jeffries's plain but respectable brown bombazine dress and plain topknot of hair. "You are not a friend of hers, no?"

Mrs. Jeffries studied the girl, wondering whether to try charm and diplomacy or bluntness and threats. The maid cocked her chin regally and started to close the door. There was no time for charm. "No, I'm not a friend, but I could be the person who helps keep your mistress from facing a hangman. So if I were you, Miss Nanette Lanier, I'd cease playing the lady of the manor and allow me in."

"How do you know my name?" Nanette exclaimed. "Who are you?"

"Who I am isn't important. Why Mrs. Leslie was hiding behind a tree in the gardens right before Dr. Bartholomew Slocum was murdered, is."

The maid cast a quick, frightened glance up the street. "You'd better step inside," she said hastily. "I theenk we need to speak together."

Nanette's accent was considerably more noticeable when she was rattled. From the pallor in her cheeks and the wariness in her blue eyes, Mrs. Jeffries knew she was indeed shaken.

She followed the maid down a hall to a small sitting room. Going inside, Nanette hurriedly closed the door and nodded toward a chair. "Please sit down," she invited. "We aren't likely to be disturbed in here. Madam Leslie is the only one who uses this room, and she's not here." She advanced toward Mrs. Jeffries and sat down on the couch opposite her. "Now, please, tell me who you are and what you want."

"My name is Hepzibah Jeffries, and I'm the housekeeper for the police inspector that questioned you and Mrs. Leslie after Dr. Slocum's murder." She ignored Nanette's gasp of surprise. "You're very loyal to Mrs. Leslie, aren't you?"

"But of course," Nanette replied. "She eez an angel. I would do anything for her. But—"

"You and your mistress both stated that on the day of the murder Mrs. Leslie hadn't left the house all day except to go onto the terrace with Dr. Hightower," Mrs. Jeffries continued, interrupting the girl. "I know for a fact that's not true. Mrs. Leslie was seen outside the Slocum house just before noon, only a few moments before the doctor was poisoned."

"But she didn't kill him," Nanette claimed passionately. "She only went over there to try and reason with him."

"Reason with a blackmailer?" Mrs. Jeffries queried softly, with a shake of her head. "Oh no, I'm afraid that was a rather foolish thing to do."

The maid's eyes widened. "How do you know she was being blackmailed?"

Mrs. Jeffries hadn't been sure until that very moment. She crossed her fingers in her lap and hoped her luck would continue.

"Dr. Slocum," she said softly, "seemed to make a habit of blackmailing his neighbors. Mrs. Leslie was only one of his victims."

"He was a terrible man and I'm glad he's dead," Nanette cried passionately. "But Mrs. Leslie didn't kill him. She eez a saint. She wouldn't hurt anyone."

"Why was he blackmailing her?"

"He wasn't," Nanette replied. "At least, he hadn't gotten any money out of her yet."

"But he was trying to."

Her shoulders slumped. "Yes. But I don't know why I should tell you about this. What business eez eet of yours?"

"Because if you don't, you'll have to tell Inspector Witherspoon, and I'm far more likely to believe you than he is. So I suggest that you trust me. If Mrs. Leslie is innocent, she has no reason to fear me."

For a few moments, the maid stared at her in silence. Finally, she spoke. "A few days before the murder, we were out in the garden and Dr. Slocum came outside." She gave a derisive laugh. "He hurried over as soon as he saw us, despite the fact that Mrs. Leslie had made it very plain she did not like him. The man had a hide like the rhinoceros. Very thick. But this time, he refused to be put off, he was very . . . how you say, forward. He insisted Madam walk with him along the path. I tried to follow, but he waved me away. I watched them walk across the garden, the doctor murmuring low in her ear and waving a little key under her nose. Suddenly, I hear her cry out. Naturally, I ran to her, but she told me to go back to the house."

"Did you?" Mrs. Jeffries asked.

Nanette shrugged. "But of course. I 'ad no choice in the matter. When Madam Leslie came inside, she was so pale I was frightened she would faint. I asked her what was wrong." She leaned forward. "You must understand, I am not just Madam Leslie's maid, I am her only confidante. She told me that Dr. Slocum threatened her. If Madam didn't give him money, he'd tell everyone that she and Dr. Hightower had murdered her husband."

Mrs. Jeffries was careful to keep her surprise from showing. "Had they?"

"*Mais non!* Excuse me, I mean, certainly not."

"Then why was Madam Leslie so worried? To be sure, it's a vicious, ugly thing to say, but if the doctor had no proof, then Mrs. Leslie or Dr. Hightower could certainly have had him up on a charge of slander. English courts do not take such matters lightly."

"That's what I told her," Nanette said earnestly. "But she claimed the doctor did have proof."

"How?" Mrs. Jeffries asked with a shake of her head. "If she and Dr. Hightower were innocent, there couldn't be any evidence."

"Oh, there was not proof of murder, but there was proof of suspicion."

"I'm afraid I don't quite follow you," Mrs. Jeffries admitted.

Nanette waved her hands in the air. "Oh, I'm explaining it so badly! This Dr. Slocum had somehow managed to obtain the medical . . . how you say . . . history, notes . . ."

"Medical records?"

"Ah yes, that eez it, medical records of Madam's late husband. This was very bad, because his own doctor, the one that wasn't there when he died, made some kind of note on these papers that Monsieur's death was odd. You see, he'd examined the man only a week earlier and found him to be in perfect health." Nanette scowled. "Bah, that only means the doctor was an idiot. But it looks very bad for Madam. It eez not the proof, but eet eez very suspicious. There eez already gossip about my dear Madam and Dr. Hightower. If something like this was spread around, especially by someone as respectable as Dr. Slocum, they would both be ruined."

Mrs. Jeffries frowned, trying to recall everything she'd heard about Mrs. Leslie. Then she remembered. "But didn't Mrs. Leslie and her husband live in Birmingham?"

"That makes no difference. Dr. Hightower happened to be there for a medical meeting. Monsieur Leslie was taken ill and his own doctor was gone. Dr. Hightower came instead.

Then poor Monsieur Leslie died suddenly." She sighed and gave a Gallic shrug. "Eet was no one's fault. Eet was the will of God. But the English, they do not understand that."

"So Slocum threatened to spread the rumor that they'd murdered her husband so they could be together," Mrs. Jeffries mused. "Yes, I can see, it all makes a nasty sort of pattern, doesn't it? But why now?"

"That eez easy to answer," Nanette said. "Madam Leslie's husband left her enough money to be comfortable, but she was not rich until now. She's an heiress. Her mama passed away recently, and she inherited everything."

"Did she tell Dr. Hightower about the blackmail attempt?"

"*Mais non,* she was too frightened. She is desperately in love with *Monsieur le Docteur,* but he has a quick temper. She was going to talk to Dr. Slocum and if that didn't work, I think she was going to pay him to keep silent."

"I see." Mrs. Jeffries's brows drew together in a puzzled frown. "But if she was just going to talk with him, why didn't she come to the front door and ask to see him? Why was she skulking around in the gardens?"

"She didn't want anyone to see her and mention it to Dr. Hightower. It is common knowledge that he loathes Dr. Slocum. So she was going to try and slip in the back door. But when she got outside his house, the butler was crossing the terrace and she didn't want him to see her. She hid behind the tree and then when the butler was gone, she couldn't go in because she heard someone in the bushes."

"Which bushes? Where?"

Nanette waved her hands toward the window. "The ones at the end of the garden, near the Seaward house. Madam was terrified by this time; she lost her nerve. So she rushed back here and told me she'd wait until her appointment to see the doctor."

"She had an appointment with him?"

"Yes, he brought his calling card around that morning. She was to see him at three o'clock that afternoon."

"Then why did she try to go over before noon?"

"Because Dr. Hightower had gotten a calling card from the doctor too," Nanette said indignantly. "He had the bad taste to actually leave it *here* when he dropped off Madam's. Dr. Hightower's appointment was for two o'clock. Madam wanted to see Dr. Slocum and try and reason with him before Dr. Hightower saw him. She was afraid of what would happen."

"Did she see who was in the bushes?"

"No, she was frightened. She fled before they came out."

Mrs. Jeffries studied the maid carefully. "You haven't told the police this, have you?"

"*Mais non!* Why would I put my mistress's neck in a noose? If I tell the police, they will think she killed him to keep him silent about her husband."

"But you must tell them, mademoiselle, you must," Mrs. Jeffries said as she rose to her feet. "And you must do it right away. I'm not the only one who knows Mrs. Lesile was in the garden right before the doctor was murdered. Inspector Witherspoon is far more likely to believe your story if you tell it voluntarily than if he finds out you've been lying."

Without waiting for an answer, she walked to the door. She turned suddenly. "Oh, and this time, I wouldn't bother with any fake hysterics."

Nanette's eyebrows rose.

Mrs. Jeffries smiled. "As a ploy, it worked once to keep the inspector from questioning your mistress too closely, but I don't think it would work twice."

Nanette looked startled for a moment, and then she laughed. "You think not, madam?" She tilted her chin to one side and regarded her out of suddenly shrewd eyes. "I thought it was rather clever of me. Especially as I was able to slip in my tidbits about Dr. Slocum's key and calling cards."

"Yes, I suspected you might have done that deliberately. Actually, it *was* rather clever. It certainly got the inspector looking elsewhere."

Nanette shrugged. "Thank you. I knew the police would find out about the cards anyway. And I hoped if they knew about the key, they would suspect someone else. Tell me, why are you here? Why are you so concerned with who killed that odious leetle man?"

Surprised by the question, Mrs. Jeffries replied without hesitation. "Because I like to help the inspector. You see, loyalty to one's employer isn't a character trait reserved solely for the French." Realizing she'd said more than she should, she quickly clamped her mouth shut.

Nanette broke into a knowing smile. "But your employer, he does not know you help him, eez that not true?"

"Well, not exactly."

The girl stared at her thoughtfully. "You can tell much about a person by his or her face. I think, madam, you have a passion for justice. You will not let them hang my mistress. Don't worry, Madam Jeffries. I will tell the inspector everything." She grinned impudently. "Except, of course, your leetle secret."

Mrs. Jeffries left by the terrace door. Nanette Lanier had sent a footman to Scotland Yard, and she knew the inspector would be along soon.

Moving quickly, she made her way to the far end and stood for a moment examining the tall, dense shrubs that composed the border on this side of the garden. Glad that she'd had the foresight to wear a sturdy pair of boots, she stepped off the path and ducked beneath a hanging branch and into the greenery.

Once inside, she stopped to get her bearings. Though the strip between the path and the border was less than ten feet wide, once you were in, you couldn't see out because of the density of the foliage. There was a good chance that whoever had been in here on the day of the murder, hadn't seen Catherine Leslie hiding behind the tree.

Slowly, her eyes on the ground, Mrs. Jeffries made her way toward Dr. Slocum's house.

As she walked, she noticed that the some of the grass was bent and many of the twigs and branches had been broken off, as though someone had been here. But that could have been the police, she reminded herself. The garden had been thoroughly searched.

The dense foliage ended at the house next to the Slocum residence. Mrs. Jeffries steeped onto the path, turned and looked back at where she'd come from. She calculated it had taken her approximately two minutes to work her way from the upper end to this spot. Interesting information, she decided reluctantly, turning toward the Slocum house, but hardly useful unless she could find that key.

Effie Beals answered the door on her first knock. "Morning, Mrs. Jeffries," the cook said with a cheery smile. "Your men's been keepin' me company till you got here."

"Good morning, Mrs. Beals," Mrs. Jeffries replied, following the woman down the passageway to the kitchen. "I hope Wiggins and Smythe haven't been a bother, but I fear that before the day is out, we'll need them."

"Course we 'aven't been a bother, Mrs. J," Smythe answered. He lifted a cup of tea in a salute. "We knows our manners."

"Been sittin' here twiddlin' our thumbs, that's what we've been doin'," Wiggins interjected mournfully. He was still put out because he hadn't had a glimpse of Miss Cannonberry in two days.

"Would you like tea?" Effie asked.

"Yes, thank you." She pulled off her gloves and took a chair at the table. "As soon as we've all had a nice cuppa, we've got to get busy."

"Doing what?" the cook asked, placing a cup of tea in front of Mrs. Jeffries.

She took a delicate sip and waited until Effie had sat down. "Is Mr. Joshua Slocum in? How many servants are here today?"

Effie snorted. "There's no one 'ere but me. Mr. Slocum's taken Keating and gone back to Colchester for his things.

Once he left, the other servants decided to scarper off. While the cat's away the mice will play."

Smythe leaned forward. "What are we lookin' for?"

"A key. I think I know what it unlocks—a strongbox. Even better, I'm fairly sure I know where it is."

They all stared at her in astonishment. Mrs. Jeffries held up her hand to belay the spate of questions she was sure was hovering on the tips of three tongues. "Time is running short. The inspector will be here soon, and we've got to find that key before he gets here." She got to her feet and turned to Wiggins. "You take the dining room, Wiggins. The key is quite small, so you've got to be sure and check inside every single object. Look under the rugs and along the curtain rails too."

Smythe leapt up. "Where do you want me to search?"

"The study. Make sure you go over the desk thoroughly; there might be a secret compartment."

"And me?" Effie stared at her uncertainly. "D'ya want me to help?"

"Yes," Mrs. Jeffries said. "Search the drawing room. Search every nook and cranny."

They searched the first floor in vain. Mrs. Jeffries pulled up carpets, peeked into oversized vases and knocked on desk drawers, looking for hidden cubbyholes until she was covered with dust.

"I don't think it's 'ere," Effie exclaimed breathlessly, as she and Smythe and Wiggins joined Mrs. Jeffries in the front hall. "We've been over this whole floor—if we didn't find it and the police didn't find it, it just ain't 'ere."

"It's got to be here," Mrs. Jeffries said firmly. "Come on, let's try a different strategy."

She led them into the dining room. "Smythe, go and sit at the head of the table and pretend to be Dr. Slocum."

Smythe raised an eyebrow and then walked to the table, pulled out a chair and sat down. "Now what?"

"Pretend you're eating lunch."

Mrs. Jeffries studied the coachman, mentally casting him

as Dr. Slocum. "All right," she murmured. "Here he is sitting, eating his lunch."

"He'd have drunk his glass of wine first," the cook interjected. "He always did. Real pig swill it was too, despite all them fancy labels."

Dutifully, Smythe pretended to drink a glass of wine.

"Yes, yes," Mrs. Jeffries murmured. "He'd have drunk the wine and then started eating the soup." Smythe pantomimed the actions as she spoke.

"Then he'd have gone on to the main course." She paused. "A few moments later, he'd have felt ill. Very ill."

She cocked her head to one side and then turned toward the door. "But he was expecting guests."

"He weren't expectin' nobody," Effie cried. "He'd given us all the day off. You don't invite a house full of people around when you don't have none 'ere to wait on 'em."

"He was expecting guests, or rather, blackmail victims. That's why he'd given the servants the day off, that's why he'd taken his calling cards around the neighborhood. That was his way of telling his victims to come along and pay up," Mrs. Jeffries said patiently.

Wiggins looked shocked. "Cor, blimey. That's a mean thing ta do ta someone."

"So here he is, feeling dreadfully ill," Mrs. Jeffries continued.

Smythe stood up and clutched his stomach. "And he had to make sure that none of them got their hands on his key." She whirled around and stared toward the hall. "So what does a doctor who's desperately and suddenly ill do?"

Before she could move, Smythe shot across the room and staggered toward the surgery. Mrs. Jeffries, Wiggins and Effie were hot on his heels.

"'E 'eads for his surgery," Smythe yelled triumphantly.

Inside the surgery, Mrs. Jeffries stopped suddenly to avoid running into the coachman. He turned, still clutching his stomach, and looked at Mrs. Jeffries. "This is as far as I can figure it," he admitted reluctantly.

"You've done very well, Smythe," she said quickly.

"Now what?" Wiggins asked.

Mrs. Jeffries studied the room. "Slocum couldn't risk anyone getting their hands on that key, so he has to hide it, and quickly."

"But we've already searched in 'ere a dozen times," Effie protested.

Mrs. Jeffries ignored her and slowly turned. The key was in here. It had to be. She stared at the neat rows of books, the medicine cabinets and supply cupboards. Frowning, she glanced at the floor. Nothing there but a Persian carpet and the doctor's medical bag leaning against the leg of a coatrack.

The medical bag. It had been sitting there since before Dr. Slocum's death.

"That's it!" she cried, dashing across the room and snatching up the bag.

"How comes the police didn't look in there?" Effie asked curiously. "They's searched the whole house."

"Because this looks like part of the furniture," Smythe answered, squatting down on his haunches. "It's been sittin' 'ere right under our noses, but because it were never mentioned and it belongs 'ere, nobody probably bothered to give it more than a quick look. Right, Mrs. J?"

"Right," she muttered. She snapped the latch and the bag popped open. "Lets see what's inside."

Bottles, pills and vials were jumbled haphazardly together in a heap beside a stack of mangled bandages. Mrs. Jeffries leaned back so Effie Beals could see the inside of the case.

"Was this normally the way the doctor kept his case?" she asked.

Effie shook her head. "I don't rightly know, but I shouldn't think so. He was generally a very particular person, didn't like a mess."

Mrs. Jeffries reached inside and began taking the contents out, one by one. Soon there was a pile of bottles, bandages and vials, but no key. Disappointment flooded her as she peered inside and saw the last object, a small flat box. She yanked it out and flipped the lid up.

"Drat," she murmured. "It's only his scalpel case." Keeping the lid open, she gently shook the case. From beneath the leather of the scalpel bed she heard a faint, but distinct thud.

"There's somethin' inside the case," Wiggins said excitedly.

Handing the case to Smythe, Mrs. Jeffries said, "Will you do the honors?"

He grinned, opened it, lifted up the instruments and the false bottom and pulled out a thin chain. At the end of the chain was a small gold key.

Wiggins shook his head. "I still can't suss out how you knew that that there key would be 'ere."

"The key had to be here," Mrs. Jeffries explained with a relieved smile. She gazed at the three puzzled faces surrounding her. "Or at least, I hoped it would be. Dr. Slocum was obsessed with money and power. Yet he had time to make his way into the surgery, get to one of his medical cupboards and try to dose himself with an emetic. But from what we know of his character, it occurred to me that before he did any of that, before he even tried to save his own life, he'd protect this key. It's not just a key to a strongbox, it's the key to his wealth and power."

Smythe shook his head admiringly, and Wiggins stared at the instrument case as if he expected it to disappear any moment.

"Where's this 'ere strongbox then?" Effie asked. "And what are we going to do when the police arrive? You said that inspector would be here any minute."

"We haven't time to worry about the strongbox now," Mrs. Jeffries said quickly. "Besides, it will be better if the inspector finds that himself." She got to her feet and turned to the cook. "Here's what I want you to say when the police arrive."

*   *   *

Less than half an hour later a rather puzzled-looking
Inspector Witherspoon followed Effie Beals into the kitchen.
As instructed, the cook had told him everything, including
the fact that Dr. Slocum was a blackmailer.

"So you see, sir," Effie continued, glancing covertly out
of the corner of her eye at the three people sitting around the
table. "When I found that key, I knew I should let you know
as quick as I could. But I were just a bit nervous, so I sent
a footman round to your house to fetch your Mrs. Jeffries.
We met the day she come here to bring you your cigar case,
and she's a right nice lady. I felt easier talkin' with you and
tellin' you about the blackmail with her 'ere."

"Yes, yes," Witherspoon replied. "I can well understand
why you'd want Mrs. Jeffries, but what on earth are Wiggins
and Smythe doing here?"

"That's my doing, Inspector," Mrs. Jeffries said calmly
as she rose from her chair.

Smythe and Wiggins got up too. "No it's not," Smythe
countered. "It's my doin'. We insisted on coming. For
protection like."

"We couldn't let her come to a 'ouse where theys been
a murder," Wiggins pointed out. "Not all alone. So we's
tagged along."

"They insisted on escorting me, Inspector, and after we
got here and heard Mrs. Beals's story, I thought you might
need them to stay. It looks as if this case of yours might
be . . . uh, taking a turn for the better."

As she spoke, she neatly maneuvered the inspector back
a step so that Smythe, Wiggins and Effie Beals could get
past him and into the hall. As she'd instructed them, they
were going up the stairs to wait for her and the inspector
outside the door of the surgery.

"Hadn't you better start searching, sir? Mrs. Beals is
almost sure that key goes to a strongbox." Mrs. Jeffries
smiled innocently.

Witherspoon sighed. "Yes, I suppose I should, and of

course, I will. But I must confess," he lowered his voice, "I'm really dreadfully tired. It's been such a day. First, the police surgeon was in a terrible state when he had to admit he'd made a mistake in the initial postmortem. Dr. Slocum didn't die from eating a poisoned mushroom, and Bainbridge is most annoyed about that. Not that I much blame him. I mean if you find a poison mushroom tidbit lying at the bottom of a chap's soup bowl, it's reasonable to assume that's how the chap died. Well, I think it's quite reasonable, but the chief inspector was livid, absolutely livid—"

Mrs. Jeffries deemed it prudent to interrupt. "I take it Dr. Slocum was poisoned?"

"Oh yes. Of course. Mrs. Beals is no longer a suspect. The woman could hardly have got hold of venom. It's not the sort of thing one finds in a kitchen."

"Venom," Mrs. Jeffries exclaimed. "What kind of venom?"

Witherspoon's footsteps slowed as they mounted the stairs. The others were already at the top. "That's another reason the doctor was upset. He couldn't tell. The body was a bit too . . . well," he grimaced, "far gone."

"I see."

"Yes, and then I got this frantic message from the Leslie household, and I had to go along there and talk to that rather snippy French maid."

Mrs. Jeffries smiled sympathetically. "Did she say anything that sheds any light on this new development?"

"I'm not sure. On the one hand, she insists that Catherine Leslie is innocent, while on the other, she tells me Mrs. Leslie was out hiding behind a tree right before Dr. Slocum was murdered. On top of that, Mrs. Leslie claims someone was hiding or walking in the bushes." He sighed dramatically as they reached the top of the stairs. "I don't know what to believe anymore."

"There, there, Inspector." Mrs. Jeffries reached over and patted his arm. "Not to worry. You'll sort it all out. You always do."

Witherspoon brightened somewhat. "Yes, I suppose I will."

They walked to the surgery and joined the trio standing in front of the door.

"I thought we might help you with your search, Inspector," Mrs. Jeffries volunteered. She smiled at Effie Beals as she threw open the doors of the surgery and led the way inside. "Wasn't it clever of Mrs. Beals to find that key?"

"What? Oh yes." The inspector looked confused. "Uh, Mrs. Jeffries, why are we here?"

"Why, Inspector, you must be jesting. Surely you know why we're here." She broke off and laughed. "Oh now, stop being so modest. This was all your idea. You told me all about it yourself."

Behind Witherspoon, she saw Smythe roll his eyes and Wiggins grin. Even Effie Beals had to turn her head to hide her smile.

"I did?" Witherspoon said. "When?"

"Don't you remember, sir? It was only a few days ago." She took his arm and steered him toward the bookcases on the other side of the surgery. "You told me that Dr. Slocum had once fired a housemaid for going near his bookcases." She pointed to the key that Witherspoon had been holding between his fingers since he'd come into the kitchen. "Mrs. Beals says that key unlocks a strongbox." She broke off and waited for him to get her point.

It took a good few minutes, but suddenly his eyes lit up like a couple of shooting stars. "By golly, I think I'm on to something here. Quick, Smythe, Wiggins, get a footstool and help me search behind the books on those top shelves. Mrs. Jeffries, you and Mrs. Beals take the lower ones."

In the end, it took less than ten minutes to find Dr. Bartholomew Slocum's strongbox. The heavy metal chest was secreted behind a set of the complete works of Mr. William Shakespeare.

CHAPTER 11

"This must be the notebook," Witherspoon said as he reached inside the strongbox and pulled out a small leather book. He flipped it open, scanned the first page and frowned. "Can't make hide nor hair of this. It's all numbers and initials."

"But Sir, this is just as you surmised. Slocum was a blackmailer. Wouldn't this be a record of payments?" Mrs. Jeffries explained. She reached over the inspector's shoulders and pointed to the top entry. "Look, DLS and right beside it, the figure 500 PQ and then the date. That's probably the initials of someone blackmailed into paying Dr. Slocum five hundred pounds every quarter."

"Egad, I believe you're right. My goodness, there's a rather lot of initials in this little book." Witherspoon ran his finger down the column, muttering to himself.

"DDI–100 PQ; LBD–225 PQ; CCS–350 PQ. Gracious, Slocum must have been blackmailing half the city."

"Wouldn't surprise me none," Effie said earnestly. "He blackmailed me into workin' for 'im. The man was capable of anythin'."

"He sounds like a right blackguard." Smythe sneered. "It's a wonder someone didn't kill 'im before now."

Witherspoon smiled wearily. "Dr. Slocum may have been a very bad man, perhaps even evil, but that doesn't give someone the right to take his life."

"Inspector, what are those?" Mrs. Jeffries pointed to the remaining papers in the strongbox.

The inspector glanced up. Effie, Smythe, Wiggins, Mrs. Jeffries and even Constable Barnes, who'd arrived just as they'd found the strongbox, were staring at the open box with avid curiosity.

Cautiously, the inspector reached inside and pulled out the stack. They were neatly folded sheets of plain white paper. On the outside of each one a name was written in precise blue ink.

He unfolded the first one, which was marked "Bradshaw". Witherspoon's expression turned grim as he read. When he'd finished, he took a deep breath, folded the paper again and placed it carefully to one side.

"What was it, sir?" Mrs. Jeffries prodded gently.

"Oh dear, I'm afraid it's the very worst. These papers are what Dr. Slocum was using to blackmail his victims. They are written records. This one," he jabbed a finger at the one he'd just put down, "is signed in the victim's own hand. It's a statement, admitting to a . . . well, youthful indiscretion."

As the inspector had turned a bright pink, Mrs. Jeffries didn't press him further. "How dreadful. Are you going to go through the rest and see if any of your suspects have one of those wretched things?"

"Hmm, yes, I expect that's exactly what I should do."

She watched as he went through the stack. Most of the names were meaningless to her. But one of them she recognized as belonging to a member of the House of Lords. Witherspoon recognized the name too, because he carefully slipped it under the bottom of the pile so the others couldn't see it.

Finally, he came to another name that was familiar to them both. Mrs. Jeffries reached over his shoulder and tapped the sheet gently. "I think that's the one you're looking for."

His hand stilled, and he glanced up and met her eye.

"Yes, Mrs. Jeffries," he agreed sadly. "I rather think it

is. After all, the murder was committed by someone who knew those wretched mushrooms were out in the garden."

Mrs. Jeffries didn't remind him that several of the blackmail victims had this information.

Inspector Witherspoon's eyes narrowed as he flipped the sheet open and began to read. Ignoring discretion, Mrs. Jeffries crowded closer to the inspector and read over his shoulder.

Witherspoon clucked his tongue softly and shook his head. "Well, what do you make of that," he muttered softly.

"A great deal," she replied briskly. "And I suspect every word of it is true. His initials were in the notebook, so we can assume he was paying."

"Hmm, yes, and he was foolish enough to sign this statement in his own hand." Witherspoon put the page facedown on the desk. "But I don't see how he could have murdered Dr. Slocum. He was with his guests."

"Who are you talking about?" Constable Barnes asked. He hadn't been close enough to the desk to see the name.

"Colonel Seaward," the inspector answered glumly.

The constable cleared his throat. "I'm not so sure he was with his guests the whole time, sir." He reached into his pocket and drew out his own small notepad. Flipping the pages, he said, "If I recall, I believe one of the footmen mentioned that the gentleman left the dining room for a few minutes. Ah yes, here it is. The lad's name is David Packard."

No longer able to contain his curiosity, Smythe asked, "Why was the colonel bein' blackmailed?"

The question galvanized Witherspoon into action. He stood up. "Colonel Seaward wasn't a hero back in that African campaign he's so famous for." He held up the paper. "This is a statement he signed admitting that he hid in a secret cellar in his quarters while his men died fighting for Queen and Country. When the reinforcements arrived, Seaward crawled out, grabbed a gun and pretended he'd been there fighting all along."

"Why would the colonel be daft enough to admit to cowardice? Especially if all the rest of 'em was dead and there weren't no one left to tell?" Wiggins asked.

"Perhaps he signed it under the influence of opium," Mrs. Jeffries answered. She turned to the inspector and smiled. "Perhaps that's how Dr. Slocum learned most of his victims' secrets. You did tell me that Slocum once treated Colonel Seaward. Don't you think it's likely he drugged the information out of him?"

"No doubt you're right," Witherspoon replied, staring at the page. "See, the signature's very wobbly. I imagine the poor man talked his head off while he was under the influence of the drug, and then Slocum made him sign this before he'd regained the use of his wits. Then he started blackmailing him."

"But sir," Constable Barnes said, "how do you know he's the murderer?" He nodded toward the desk. "Looks to me like there's a whole heap of suspects now."

Witherspoon clasped his hands together and frowned. He was thinking.

Mrs. Jeffries decided it was time to intervene. "Well, of course he's the one, and Inspector Witherspoon can prove it."

The inspector gave her a puzzled frown. "Eh?"

"Oh sir, don't be so self-effacing. Why, you were the one that pointed out the significance of that piece of cork we stumbled onto here in the surgery."

"Yes, I suppose I did." He looked very confused now.

She gave him a confident smile. "Now, don't tell me, let me guess. Your next step will be to send Constable Barnes over to bring that footman here. Once the lad is here, you'll confirm precisely how long the colonel was actually gone. Am I right, sir?"

"Of course," Witherspoon gave himself a slight shake. "Of course," he repeated more forcefully, "that's exactly what I was going to do. Barnes, go get the lad."

She waited till the constable left before continuing. "And then you'll send Smythe along to the Yard to get the bottle Dr. Slocum drank from on the day he died. Correct?"

Witherspoon smiled uncertainly. "Uh, yes." He turned to the coachman. "Smythe, would you pop along to the Yard for me? It's just as Mrs. Jeffries says; I want you to get that wine bottle. It's in the evidence box."

Smythe nodded. "Do you want me to bring it here?"

"Yes." The inspector broke off as he suddenly realized what to do. "I mean, no. Before you come back, stop at the wine merchant's, the big one on the corner. Give the bottle to Constable Barnes. He'll question the proprietor to see if they have a record of who they sold that bottle to." Pausing, he reached into his pocket for his notebook, scribbled a quick note and handed it to Smythe. "Use this to get the Yard to release the bottle into your custody. Barnes will be waiting for you at the corner."

Relief swept over Mrs. Jeffries as she realized that the inspector was finally seeing the probable sequence of events. There was only one way the murder could have been committed. She'd known that since last night. Now, she knew why.

"Come on, boy," Effie said to Wiggins. "Let's go down to the kitchen for a cuppa. There's nothin' we can do here but get in the way."

"Do I have to?" Wiggins complained, looking at Mrs. Jeffries. "It's just now gettin' interestin'."

"I think so," she replied softly. "We'll call you when we need you."

After they'd gone, Mrs. Jeffries turned to the inspector. "I suppose it was learning that the doctor had died of venom poisoning that made you realize the murderer could only be Colonel Seaward."

Actually, the inspector hadn't even thought of the cause of death until Mrs. Jeffries mentioned it. But now that she had, he quickly saw the connection.

"Naturally. As soon as the police surgeon said the word 'venom,' I understood everything."

"You're so very clever, sir."

"Not really." He laughed modestly. "There's only one person in this case who has access to any kind of venom at all. Colonel Seaward. I think I must have begun to suspect he was the killer when Nanette Lanier claimed that Mrs. Leslie had heard someone in the bushes right before the doctor was murdered. After seeing that," he nodded at the paper on the desk, "I knew for certain. In case you didn't know it, Mrs. Jeffries, Colonel Seaward is quite a well-known amateur naturalist. He's the only suspect who not only had access to venom, but would have had the skill to extract it as well."

Mrs. Jeffries was quite impressed. Though the inspector often appeared baffled by his cases, he was quite capable when it came right down to it. "What led you to the conclusion that the poison was snake venom? I thought the police surgeon wasn't sure."

"He isn't. But it could hardly have been bee venom, not this time of year, and I don't think it was a scorpion or a poisonous spider. Contrary to what most people think, those poisons aren't always lethal, but some snake venom is."

The door opened. Constable Barnes and a dark-haired young man wearing the livery of a footman entered. "Here's the lad, sir."

The boy nodded nervously as the introductions were completed.

After the preliminary questions concerning the day of the murder were done with, Witherspoon got right to the point. "Now, I know you've stated that Colonel Seaward was with his guests from eleven till two, but wasn't there a period where he left for a few minutes?"

"No," the boy replied hesitantly. "I don't think so, sir."

"Now, lad," Constable Barnes cautioned, "we're talkin' about a murder here. Don't you remember tellin' me that the colonel nipped out for a bit to fetch a bottle of wine?"

"Oh, that. But he was only gone a few minutes."

Witherspoon began pacing the floor. "How many minutes?"

"Well, I wasn't watching the clock, sir," the footman protested. "So I don't know exactly."

"Yes, yes," the inspector said soothingly. "I can understand that, but surely you can estimate how long he was gone."

The boy chewed on his lower lip. "It was perhaps five, maybe six minutes."

"But it could have been as long as seven or eight minutes? Is that possible?" Witherspoon stopped in front of the footman and fixed him with a hard stare.

"I suppose so," he admitted reluctantly.

"Good." Witherspoon turned toward Barnes. "That'll be all. Take the lad back and then pop over to the wine merchant's. My coachman will meet you there—he'll have the wine bottle the victim drank from. Check the records and get a confirmation as to whom that bottle of wine was actually sold to."

"Right, sir." Barnes and the footman started to walk to the door.

"Just a moment," Witherspoon called. They both turned. "Does Colonel Seaward have any poisonous snakes in his collection?"

"Several, sir," the boy said, looking surprised. "But he keeps them in Surrey. He's got two cobras from Africa and a great big rattler from the United States."

"Fine. Thank you. Carry on, Constable."

As soon as they'd left, Mrs. Jeffries said, "I must admit it's so exciting to watch you work. What will you do next?"

She wondered if she should tell him about her own excursion into the foliage at the end of the garden. Going slowly, it had taken her two minutes to get from the Seaward house to Dr. Slocum's.

"What will I be doing next?" he repeated. He gazed around the surgery, his expression mirroring his uncertainty.

Mrs. Jeffries decided he needed a few more nudges.

"Why don't you take Wiggins, sir?" she suggested cheerfully. "I think he feels left out."

Witherspoon cocked his chin to one side. "Take Wiggins where?"

"Why, to the gardens." She gave a disappointed sigh. "Oh dear, don't tell me I've guessed wrong. I felt sure you'd go out into all that dense foliage at the far end and time how long it took to get from here to the Seaward house."

Witherspoon stared at her for a moment and then blinked.

"Now, now," he said, reaching over and patting her hand. "Don't look so disappointed. Your guess was most accurate. That's precisely what I intend to do. And taking Wiggins is a good idea. He can hold my watch."

While Wiggins and Witherspoon were in the garden, Mrs. Jeffries tried to decide whether or not to tell the inspector about Joshua Slocum and Keating. He hadn't mentioned speaking with either man.

A few minutes later, she heard footsteps in the hall and decided to say nothing. What good would it do? Joshua Slocum had really only stolen from himself. Scotland Yard had more important matters to concern themselves with.

"One minute and forty seconds," Witherspoon announced as he and Wiggins came into the surgery.

"How interesting," Mrs. Jeffries said. "Then it's entirely possible for Seaward to have gone through the bushes unseen, climbed into the open window in the kitchen, rushed up here," she paused and walked to the cabinet they'd found the piece of cork under, "and propped the wine bottle he'd taken from his own cellar up here." She pantomimed the gestures as she spoke. "Wiggins, watch the time. But in his rush, he pushed too hard on the corkscrew, which I suspect he had hidden in his coat. When he pulled the cork out, it disintegrated and he didn't notice. Then he added the poison, which he'd also secreted somewhere on his person . . ." She turned suddenly and dashed for the dining room. Witherspoon and Wiggins were right behind her.

"He snatched the wine Keating had put here for the doctor's lunch," she continued as she walked to the table. "And then added the poison mushroom bits he'd taken from the garden to the soup bowl. On his way out, he dropped the other poison mushroom into the bowl of edible mushrooms so that it would look like an accident or as if someone else had done the murder." She turned to Wiggins. "How long did that take?"

"Two minutes."

"So he had more than enough time," Witherspoon mused. "And now we know what his motive was."

"I reckon he got tired of payin' up," Wiggins said helpfully.

"Oh no, Wiggins," Witherspoon replied. "His motive was far more complex than that. No doubt Slocum knew about the upcoming appointment. I believe I mentioned it to you, Mrs. Jeffries. Seaward was in line for a very high position in the service of the Crown . . ."

She pretended to look confused for a moment. "Why, yes. How astute of you to make the connection."

Wiggins scratched his chin. "Make what connection?"

Before the inspector could answer, the door flew open and Smythe and Constable Barnes burst in. Barnes held up the wine bottle.

"You were right, sir. This bottle wasn't sold to Dr. Slocum; it was sold to Colonel Clayton Seaward. The proprietor keeps excellent records, he does. Likes to make sure he has what his customers want on hand. This here is fine wine, much better than the swill he sold Dr. Slocum."

"Right, then." Witherspoon started for the door. "We'd better go and ask the colonel a few questions. Constable, bring the bottle. The sight of it may loosen the gentleman's tongue."

"But, Inspector," Barnes cried, "Colonel Seaward isn't there anymore. When I took the lad back, the butler told me the colonel had left for his estate in Surrey right. He scarpered right off as soon as we brought young David over for questioning."

"Damn—oh, excuse me, Mrs. Jeffries," he said apologetically. "That kind of language is unpardonable, especially in front of a lady."

"Please, sir, it's quite all right. Believe me, I do understand. What will you do now?"

Witherspoon started pacing. "Oh dear, oh dear. I wonder if he suspects we're on to him?" Suddenly he stopped and looked at the coachman. "Smythe, there's no time to lose. How quickly can those horses of ours get us to Surrey?"

"With me driving, Bow and Arrow can beat about any set of nags on the road," Smythe said proudly. "But the colonel's got a good 'ead start."

Witherspoon nodded and turned to his housekeeper. "Mrs. Jeffries, I hate to burden you with this, but would you be kind enough to take the strongbox and its contents back to Upper Edmonton Gardens?" He smiled gently. "I'll feel better knowing it's in safe hands."

She was touched by his trust. "Of course, Inspector."

"Come on then," he said to Barnes and Smythe as he raced to the door. "Let's get cracking. Oh, and Wiggins, you're to escort Mrs. Jeffries home. Guard her and that box with your life."

"Yes, sir," Wiggins shouted as they disappeared out the door.

Despite a hair-raising ride to Seaward's estate, by the time they found the open gates leading to the house, they were a good hour behind their suspect.

Smythe slapped the reins as the horses raced up the curved driveway and the carriage took the bend on two wheels.

"Egad, do try and get us there in one piece," Witherspoon shouted as the carriage bounced hard back onto the ground.

"Yes, sir." Smythe pulled powerfully on the brake as the house came into view. When they'd jolted to a sharp stop, he jumped down off the seat and flung open the carriage door. "Do you want me to come in, Inspector?"

Witherspoon's bowler was askew, and Barnes's ruddy complexion was pale.

"There's only the two of us, sir," the constable pointed out. "Perhaps it would be a good idea for your coachman to accompany us."

"Yes, I expect you're right."

They crossed the porch, and Barnes, still holding the wine bottle clutched to his chest, used his other hand to bang the knocker hard.

A tall, white-haired butler answered the door. "Yes?"

"We'd like to see Colonel Seaward," Witherspoon began.

"Are you the police?"

Puzzled, the inspector nodded. The butler opened the door wider and ushered them inside.

"Colonel Seaward is expecting you," he said, leading the way down the hall. "It's right this way."

Confused, they looked at one another as they followed the butler through a set of double doors and into the study.

"Ah, Inspector Witherspoon, good to see you, sir. I've been waiting for you." Colonel Seaward, holding a glass of what looked like whiskey in his hand, rose from behind a desk as the three men advanced across the polished hardwood floors.

Witherspoon swallowed nervously. Now that he was here, he wasn't precisely sure how he should approach the matter.

"Good day, sir. I'm dreadfully sorry to disturb you, but I've some rather pertinent questions to ask you." He nodded to his companions. "This is Constable Barnes, whom I believe you've met, and this is . . . 'er . . . my coachman."

Seaward gazed at them blankly; then his attention focused on the bottle in Barnes's hands. For a moment, he simply stared at it; then he sucked in a long breath of air and expelled it in a sharp hiss.

"I shouldn't worry about asking me any questions, Inspector," Seaward said sadly. He smiled slightly, lifted the glass to his lips and drained it in one long gulp.

"I'm not worried, sir . . . ," Witherspoon said hesitantly. This was the most confusing situation. The man was acting decidedly odd.

Seaward put down the glass, picked up a paper from the desk and handed it to Witherspoon. "Everything you need to know is right here."

Startled, he took the sheet. As he read the small, neat handwriting, the inspector's eyes widened. When he finished, he looked up and met the other man's eyes.

Witherspoon was so stunned he found it difficult to speak. When he could find his voice, he said, "Good Lord, man. Do you know what you've done? This is a confession."

Seaward laughed harshly. "Naturally. I'm not a fool. I knew as soon as your constable came for the footman that you were on to me. So I decided to save Her Majesty's Police Force a great deal of time and trouble. Thoughtful of me, isn't it?"

Witherspoon straightened his spine and cleared his throat. "Colonel Clayton Seaward, I'm arresting you for the murder of Dr. Bartholomew Slocum. This confession will be used in evidence against you at your trial. Do you understand that?"

"Trial?" Seaward laughed again. "There won't be a trial," he said. "That was rather thoughful of me too."

And then he doubled over.

Witherspoon, Barnes and Smythe all moved at once. They scrambled around the desk, trying to grab the stricken man.

Smythe reached him first and gently lowered him into the chair. "Cor, guv', take it easy. Let's get ya into this chair."

"Barnes, call for a doctor," Witherspoon ordered. But before the constable could move, Seaward held up his hand.

"It's too late for that," he murmured. "I've meted out my own punishment. I'll die the way I killed him."

"Go on, man," the inspector shouted as the constable hesitated. "Take the coach and get the nearest doctor." Barnes ran for the door.

Seaward moaned and shook his head. "It won't do any good. I'll be dead before he gets here. I made sure of that. The venom of the cape cobra is the most toxic of all." He groaned and let out a strangled gasp.

"My God," Smythe muttered, as he stared at the colonel's face. "Poor, stupid bastard."

Seaward's body was starting to swell, and his skin was whitening as the seconds ticked past. "The cobra's in the conservatory," he rasped. "Seven feet long, nasty little creature. Have your men take care when they . . ." He broke off, clutched his chest and slumped forward onto the desk.

But it was another hour before he died. Witherspoon was glad the man had, mercifully, been unconscious.

"So you see," the inspector said proudly. "Once the footman told us that Seaward kept poisonous snakes out at his country place, well, the solution was as clear as the nose on your face."

"But I still don't understand what them mushrooms had to do with it," Betsy said.

Mrs. Goodge, Wiggins, Betsy, Smythe and Mrs. Jeffries were all sitting around the kitchen table listening to Inspector Witherspoon's brilliant resolution of the case.

The inspector and Smythe had arrived back late in the evening, so late that Mrs. Jeffries had almost worn a hole in the floor with her pacing. But when they finally arrived, shocked but unharmed, she'd insisted everyone sit down to a nice cup of hot chocolate.

Witherspoon had been talking nonstop ever since.

"Well, you see, Betsy," he continued, reaching for another currant bun, "the mushrooms were really the key to the whole mystery. I expect it was when Colonel Seaward heard Mrs. Crookshank shouting about those poisonous mushrooms that he came up with his plan."

Wiggins wrinkled his nose. "Why didn't he use one of them to kill the doctor? Why go to all the trouble of gettin' snake venom?" He shuddered.

"Because mushrooms aren't nearly as reliable as venom," Witherspoon explained. "Furthermore, Colonel Seaward was an avid naturalist. His butler admitted he was very skilled at milking snakes. But when he knew about the mushrooms, he saw his opportunity. If the doctor died of mushroom poisoning, there was a good chance the death would be ruled accidental. Snake venom without a snake is rarely considered accidental."

"So let me see if I've got this right," Mrs. Goodge said. "Colonel Seaward heard about them mushrooms on Saturday at Mrs. Crookshank's tea party."

"That's right," Witherspoon agreed. "Then he went to Surrey. On Wednesday morning, he milked the snake and brought the venom back."

Smythe leaned forward. "But 'ow did he know Slocum would be alone that day?"

"Well," Witherspoon hesitated, "he didn't know for certain until Slocum dropped his calling card by. That was Slocum's way of notifying his victims to come along and pay up. That's why none of the servants were ever present."

"How come Seaward didn't just pay up?" Betsy asked. "'E's a rich man and he'd been paying for a bloomin' long time. Why risk committin' a murder?"

"I knows that one," Wiggins interjected proudly. "He was gettin' that appointment from the Queen. He didn't want nuthin' interferin' with that, right?" He looked at the inspector.

"Yes, that's it exactly. In the confession, he admitted that he'd been paying Slocum blackmail money. He also said he feared that money wasn't going to be enough. Slocum didn't just want cash anymore; he wanted acceptance and access into Colonel Seaward's circle of friends and acquaintances. Seaward, of course, couldn't risk that. Not only did Slocum know about the African incident, but he was disreputable enough that I'm sure the colonel feared he'd try his nasty blackmailing tricks on others. No true gentleman would want to expose his friends to a person like that."

Mrs. Jeffries thought that a "true gentleman" wouldn't commit a murder either. "Do you honestly think that's why Seaward killed him?" she asked softly. "To save his friends?"

Witherspoon looked thoughtful. "I don't really know. I'd like to think so."

Betsy frowned. "But why'd he kill himself? You told us when you first come in that the case against him was pretty circum . . ."

"Circumstantial?" the inspector supplied helpfully. "It was, but we could have made a case and Seaward knew that. Once we knew what to look for, Dr. Bainbridge would have found evidence that Slocum had died of cape cobra venom. We already had the statement from the wine merchant confirming that the bottle of wine found in the Slocum house was one that Seaward had purchased, and we would have had the footman's testimony that the colonel was away from his guests long enough to have committed the murder." He shrugged. "But as to why he took his own life, I expect he couldn't face the disgrace. It would have all come out. Blackmail, Africa, being a coward."

"I reckon it's all for the best," Mrs. Goodge said. "Even with all that evidence, he still might 'ave gotten off, and that wouldn'a been right."

"I don't think so," Mrs. Jeffries countered. "He was the only one with a truly compelling motive. Effie Beals didn't have to kill the doctor; she was getting ready to leave for Australia. Dr. Hightower couldn't have done it, because he hadn't heard about Slocum's attempt to blackmail Mrs. Leslie. Slocum was already dead when Hightower arrived and found the body."

"What about Mrs. Leslie?" Mrs. Goodge protested. "She 'ad a right good motive."

"She also has the backbone of a spineless chicken," Mrs. Jeffries argued. "I don't think that woman would have the gumption to say boo to a goose, let alone kill a man."

Everyone laughed, and the impromptu little gathering broke up. As soon as Witherspoon had disappeared up the stairs, Mrs. Jeffries turned to the others.

"Well, we've done it. We've helped our inspector solve another case." She smiled broadly. "You should all be very proud of yourselves. Each and every one of you made an extremely valuable contribution. Because of your efforts, an innocent woman will be able to leave these shores for a new life."

Wiggins yawned. Betsy stood up and stretched. Smythe checked the time to see if the pub was still open, and Mrs. Goodge stuffed the last of the currant buns into her mouth.

"Well, really," Mrs. Jeffries protested. "Here I am trying to hand round compliments and you lot can't be bothered to listen."

"Don't take it wrong, Mrs. J," Smythe said as he headed for the door. "But time's a-wastin', and I ain't been for a quick one in two days."

"Oh no," Betsy said soothingly, "we're just a tad tired tonight. You can compliment us all you want tomorrow. We just can't take it all in tonight." She gave another mighty stretch. "*I'm* all in. I'm for bed."

"Frettin' and worryin' is hard work," Mrs. Goodge pointed out. "And we've done our fair share this afternoon and tonight. Why don't you save that pretty little speech till tomorrow when we can all appreciate it like?"

Mrs. Jeffries shook her head and went up to the drawing room. She understood what they were trying to tell her. They were tired, both emotionally and physically. And so was she.

As she passed the drawing room, she saw the inspector kneeling in front of the fireplace. He was building a fire. She hesitated just inside the door and watched as the match flared and the flames caught.

"Inspector Witherspoon," she called softly.

He turned slightly, and she saw what he was doing. "Mrs. Jeffries, do come in."

Dr. Slocum's strongbox was opened. Witherspoon began feeding in the papers, one by one. Slowly, Mrs. Jeffries walked to the hearth.

She stopped beside him.

"I won't burn Colonel Seaward's statement," he said, as he tossed another paper into the flames. "That's evidence. But I really didn't think it was *right* for the indiscretions of many innocent people to be in the possession of the Metropolitan Police."

"I see."

He looked up at her, his eyes pleading for her to understand. "Do you think I'm doing the right thing, Mrs. Jeffries?"

"Oh yes," she answered with a smile. "I think you're doing exactly the right thing."

Epilogue

Mrs. Jeffries put the last of the clean sheets in the linen closet, tucked in a few dewberry-scented wood chips and closed the door. She stood in the hallway for a few moments, wishing she had something to do next more interesting than going over the shopping lists with Mrs. Goodge.

But she didn't have anything particularly interesting to do. She hadn't had anything particularly interesting to do since they'd discovered Dr. Slocum's murderer over three weeks ago. Mrs. Jeffries thought that was a miserable state of affairs.

And from the way the rest of the household has been acting, she mused as she trudged down the stairs, they all agreed with that sentiment.

Not that the case hadn't ended satisfactorily, she told herself as she paused on the third-floor landing. It had.

The Home Office had quietly congratulated the inspector on another brilliant investigation, while at the same time they buried any news reports regarding the matter so deep a mole couldn't find them. That annoyed Mrs. Jeffries. She thought that possible embarrassment to Her Majesty was a decidedly stupid reason for manipulating an alledgely free press. But there was little she could do about it.

As she reached the bottom of the steps, she decided she was being foolish. She and the rest of the household had to get back into their routine. Everyone at Upper Edmonton Gardens was suffering from a bad case of the doldrums, and it had to stop.

Betsy was so bored she'd taken to reading the obituaries every day on the off chance that she'd come across something suspicious. Mrs. Goodge's cooking had deteriorated, Smythe had stopped going to the pub, and even Wiggins couldn't be bothered to hang about out front and watch for Miss Cannonberry.

They were all being far too self-indulgent. Why, one couldn't expect always to have a nice little mystery to sink one's teeth in.

As she passed the drawing room, Mrs Jeffries popped her head in and checked the time. She smiled. They'd all be in the kitchen having tea. This was as good a time as any to tell them to stop feeling sorry for themselves.

Well . . . She paused and decided that maybe she'd wait till tomorrow to deliver her lecture. Perhaps today they'd all go out for a nice treat somewhere. That would cheer everyone up.

Mrs. Jeffries was halfway down the back stairs when she heard the laughter. She hurried into the kitchen and then came to a full stop.

The table was set for an elaborate tea. Mrs. Goodge had used the good china and a linen tablecloth. She'd put out cakes and buns and plates of dainty sandwiches.

But that wasn't what made Mrs. Jeffries blink with surprise.

Luty Belle Crookshank was sitting at the head of the table as if she were the Queen of Sheba. She'd just made some comment that had Smythe roaring with laughter, Betsy giggling and Wiggins grinning from ear to ear. Even Mrs. Goodge was smiling.

"Hello there, Hepzibah," Luty shouted as she caught sight of her. "I was wonderin', if you was of a mind to join us."

"Luty Belle," Mrs. Jeffries exclaimed as she came to the

table. "This is certainly a delightful surprise. I'm so happy to see you."

Luty cackled. "I'm mighty glad to be here. I was just tellin' everybody about how I was watchin' them gardens during the Slocum trouble."

"Really," Mrs. Jeffries said cautiously.

Luty cackled again. "Now, Hepzibah. Don't go gettin' stiff on me. But a body'd have to be blind not to notice you lot out there prancin' about and askin' questions."

Everyone at the table went utterly still. Betsy's eyes were as wide as saucers, Smythe was watching the elderly lady the way a fox eyes a chicken, Wiggins had ceased chewing on a slice of Battenburg cake, and Mrs. Goodge's hand had stopped halfway to the teapot.

Mrs. Jeffries decided to brazen it out. "Why, Luty Belle, I haven't the faintest notion what you're talking about."

"Good bluff," Luty said admiringly. "Did ya ever play poker? I bet you'd have been doggone good at it. But that's not why I'm here."

Mrs. Jeffries smiled politely. "I thought this was a social call."

Luty Belle shook her head. "Nope. Mind ya, now that I've been and had a good time, I'll be sure to come again. But I really came because I thought you—" She broke off and looked around the table. "And the rest of ya— could give me a little help."

"If'n you're offerin' us a job," Smythe said, "we're sorry, but we's happy here."

"It's a job all right," Luty replied with a vigorous shake of her head. "But it's not what you're a thinkin'. You see, I saw the ways all of you helped solve ol' Slocum's murder. Got sharp eyes, I have. You lot were all over that neighborhood, asking questions, and even better, you was gettin' answers."

"Luty Belle," Mrs. Jeffries interrupted. "What is this all about?" Her spirits were lifting by the second, but she didn't want to get her hopes too high.

Luty sighed, and all traces of amusement left her face.

"Well," she said softly, "I've got me this problem and I think I need some help. I was hoping you all could give me a hand."

EARLENE FOWLER

Introduces Benni Harper, curator of San Celina's folk art museum and amateur sleuth

> **Each novel is named after a quilting pattern that is featured in the story.**

"Benni's loose, friendly, and bright. Here's hoping we get to see more of her..."–<u>The Kirkus Reviews</u>

__FOOL'S PUZZLE 0-425-14545-X/$4.99

Ex-cowgirl Benni Harper moved from the family ranch to San Celina, California, to begin a new career as curator of the town's folk art museum. But one of the museum's first quilt exhibit artists is found dead. And Benni must piece together an intricate sequence of family secrets and small-town lies to catch the killer.

"Compelling...Keep a lookout for her next one."
                    –<u>Booklist</u>

__IRISH CHAIN   0-425-15137-9/$5.50

When Brady O'Hara and his former girlfriend are murdered at the San Celina Senior Citizen's Prom, Benni believes it's more than mere jealousy. She decides to risk everything–her exhibit, her romance with police chief Gabriel Ortiz, and ultimately her life–uncovering the conspiracy O'Hara had been hiding for fifty years.